First published by Primal Instinct 2024

This novel is entirely a work of fiction. The names, characters and incidents portrayed in it are the work of the author's imagination. Any resemblance to actual persons, living or dead, events or localities is entirely coincidental.

Nelle Nikole asserts the moral right to be identified as the author of this work.

Nelle Nikole has no responsibility for the persistence or accuracy of URLs for external or third-party Internet Websites referred to in this publication and does not guarantee that any content on such Websites is, or will remain, accurate or appropriate.

Designations used by companies to distinguish their products are often claimed as trademarks. All brand names and product names used in this book and on its cover are trade names, service marks, trademarks and registered trademarks of their respective owners. The publishers and the book are not associated with any product or vendor mentioned in this book. None of the companies referenced within the book have endorsed the book.

Editing: EJL Editing & Crab Editing

Cover: MiblArt

Maps: cartographybird

Before Their After

A State of the Union Novella Collection

Nelle Nikole

WORLD OF RISING

PLAYLIST

To those who choose to keep fighting, I see you.

Author Note

Hi, it's me, Nelle. Just wanted to take a minute to pop in to explain what you can expect to find in this little prequel of mine.

Before Their After is just that, the before to The After you follow our band of misfits through in Rising and throughout the series. These are stories about what made our crew, what shaped them, how they became who they are 'today.' Some are fun, some are traumatic. Some fall somewhere in between. A glance behind the curtain, if you will. Each section falls independent on itself but ties into the larger story. So sit back, grab your coffee and pie, get cozy, and enjoy.

xo,

Nelle

Recommended Reading Order

Option 1: The World Builder

1. Before Their After
2. Rising
3. Echoes of War

This is for you if you:

- Enjoy a good background on characters.
- Like easing into a new world.
- Hate going back in time.

Option 2: The Empath

1. Rising
2. Echoes of War

3. Before Their After

This if for you if you:

- Like tears.
- Need to feel something, good or bad.
- Like reading in publication order.

OPTION 3: THE MOOD READER

1. Rising
2. Before Their After
3. Echoes of War

This if for you if you:

- Need a moment to process everything.

PART ONE
DAY 0

No Phones

AMAIA

Forever is not infinite.

The two terms are similar in the way humanity has come to understand them, yes. But at their base, they are different. Forever is practical. The idea that I will care about the ones I've loved and lost far into the future. As long as my mind can conceptualize the idea of love, then the love I hold for them will always exist.

Forever has limitations, whereas infinite does not. Through time and through space, when our names are long forgotten by any human left, that love would still exist. Forever is foundational. You can build off it. Use it to power you. Infinite is limitless. Infinite love will have you burn the village down at the risk of your own safety.

What makes a soldier? How does one become a monster? What turns a person into the villain from their darkest dreams? Changes them, molds them until they no longer recognize who they'd become.

Life doesn't stop the moment the worst thing in your life happens. It keeps moving and you mold yourself into the person you need to be in order to survive. These were the questions and thoughts I'd theorize over as I read my favorite stories every night before bed. You see, the mind can take you anywhere. On countless adventures to explore your wildest thoughts. I was a dreamer. An optimist in the worst of situations, always imagining what could be.

Perhaps that's why I never gave up. Maybe that is why when my reality shattered, I kept pushing, never let myself settle with the truth of my reality. When the world around you changes in an instant, it's hard to settle and let life catch up. That infinite love, the desire to keep living on when they cannot, is fueling.

"You are not wearing a white suit," I teased, stabbing at an eel roll and plopping it into my mouth with a moan.

It'd been the first time I'd had a chance to eat all day. Traffic had been terrible on the way to work, making it impossible to stop for my morning coffee. Then the emails hadn't slowed and anything further than the vending machine was unattainable. Xavier made up for it, though. He always did. Tonight was wedding planning night, and he'd stopped at our favorite sushi place on his way home. All waiting for me with a fresh vase of flowers and a freshly baked pie on the counter upon my arrival.

Harley whined as Xavier took a seat next to me on the

couch. The cedar-scented body wash from his shower had me shifting closer under his arm. He reached down to scratch behind Harley's ear. "Why not?"

"Because it doesn't match the vibes of a barn wedding," I said, using my chopsticks to fight off his wandering fingers on my plate.

"Maia," he sighed as his dark brown fingers rubbed against his temples. "We are not getting married in a barn."

I rolled my eyes, leaning into his chest. "You're right ... I'm not thinking big enough. We should totally do the—"

"Redwoods," Sloan and I said in unison, erupting into laughter.

Xavier groaned, clicking on the corner of the phone and finding Sloan's face on the screen. "Hi, Sloan. This is going to cost me a pretty penny, isn't it?"

"I'd say she's worth it, but hey, that's just me!"

"You don't count, Sloan," he said, glaring into the phone. "I want to talk to my future wife alone now, if you don't mind. Bye-bye."

He clicked the end button, setting my phone and plate on the coffee table.

"Hey!" I shouted, but his hand cupping my chin silenced me as he leaned in for a kiss.

"Wedding planning night." Xavier leaned away, leveling a stare before coming back for another peck. "No phones."

"That was wedding planning," I chuckled, knowing the vibrating phone on the table was from one of my girls.

He grabbed it, typing in the password and reading the most recent text out loud. "Sloan: For bridesmaids dresses I'm thinkin' olive green. My baby cousin did this color profile thing on me and it looks fantastic against my skin."

I shrugged. "It does look really good on her—"

"That is not wedding planning," he interrupted, grabbing a piece of my sushi while I was distracted. I smacked his arm before stealing a sip of his beer in turn. "Sammy: Green washes me out. No green."

"It's as much wedding planning as my brain can take at the moment, I'll tell you that." I groaned. So much to do, so little time. There were never enough hours in the day, it seemed.

Xavier's brown eyes reflected the screen as he typed a response. "There. Problem solved." He tossed my phone onto the rug and out of reach and switched the TV to display his 'wedding planning' PowerPoint.

"What did you do?" I asked, my laugh caught in my throat as he swooped me into his lap.

The constant buzz of my phone hummed in the distance as we debated over different venues and how they fit into our budget. He'd been oddly thorough. More than I'd expected, considering most of my friends who'd gotten married complained about doing it all on their own.

Now I was scrolling through Pinterest on his laptop.

"I honestly don't think it'll rain. But if you insist, it appears they have a contingency plan. Not as cute, but like I said, it's not going to rain," I called out to him from the snug little corner of our studio apartment.

The toilet flushed in the bathroom and I took the moment to check my phone. Harley's ears perked up as I unlocked the screen.

"What is it, girl?" I asked, rubbing the spot near her back legs that often calmed her down.

The vase of flowers crashed off the bar cart. I turned around, Xavier's brown skin a sickly green color. One hand fell over his stomach, the other grasping his chiming phone. "Something's ... wrong."

"What? Like bad sushi or something?" I stood up, crossing the room. The continued buzzing of my phone fought for my attention. My heart stopped the moment I glanced down. The first text on my phone in a string of notifications from friends and news stations alike.

Dad: Day 0. Stay safe. We love you.

"Xavier—" I started, looking up to find him making his way to the ground.

His head slammed into the hardwood floor, body convulsing. The brown eyes I'd become accustomed to glazed over, unseeing as he stared up at me, his body utterly still. "Xavier!" I shouted, pushing Harley back as she pried her way between us.

With the twitch of his head, the tension in my body eased. *Alive. He's still alive.* Until his gaze connected with mine. The only force stronger than love is fear. Maybe that's why I ran.

One Last Ride

REINA

I'd spent so much of the last few years wishing on every passing star and plane to have more moments like this. The three of us, the laughter of my brothers, full and hearty in the distance as I kept to my own. Just the energy around them was enough to make me somewhat happy to be content with this little life of mine.

Seth had been gone for far too long. The gap in his presence was felt by us all. I didn't blame him for any of it. We all reacted in different ways. If he had to run away to get better, then so be it, as long as he found his way back to us. Warm sunlight streamed into the stables, highlighting the little white speckles of dust in its glow. I tapped my foot against the wooden stool to the beat of some song on my 'Good Vibes Only' playlist, humming along to the harmony, my fingers weaving knots into a crochet top.

A bucket of water clanged against the floor, startling me into a straightened posture. Hunter lay on his ass with a menacing glare at Seth's pointed finger. I grinned, joining in Seth's rare laugh, and shook my head at Hunter's clumsiness. Though I wasn't exactly coordinated, Hunter was less than balanced himself unless he was on top of a horse, which seemed to be more time than not these days.

"I knew that was behind me," he grumbled, but took Seth's extended hand. Hunter brushed himself off as Seth mounted his horse. "Wanna go for a ride, little sister?"

I dropped my crochet hook, leaning forward as I looked them over and tried not to appear too eager. "You sure I won't just slow y'all down?"

"Probably," Seth mumbled, staring down at me from the top of his horse, Freedom. My brother was already tall, and gazing up at him on the seat of his stallion put a crook in my neck. Heat rushed to my cheeks as I glanced at Hunter, then picked at my crochet hook. Hunter cleared his throat, mounting his mare without tearing his hard stare from his twin. "But that doesn't mean we don't want you to come."

Clicking pause on my tunes, I stopped what I was doing and quickly tied my hair into a braid. Hunter reached out a hand before I crossed over to his horse's stall. "Up you go. Ride with me, for old times' sake?"

A toothy smile wide enough to pinch my cheeks took

over. I hadn't been for a ride with Hunter in ages. Since we were kids, actually. It was a memory I dreamed about when my family was falling apart. I used to spend a lot of time with my brothers. Then James died and Seth left. The loss of them both had sent Hunter into a period of recluse, leaving me to my lonesome.

Riding the property in one of the trucks or a four-wheeler was one thing. Feeling the rhythmic motion of Hunter's sweet Daisy beneath me, her muscles flexing with each step, was a beauty of its own. I'd forgotten how picturesque the rolling hills of Billings were. They resembled a dang painting that cost thousands of dollars hanging in some fancy museum. Green grass waved in the breeze in every direction. The blue of the sky seemed brighter accompanied by the earthy aroma of the rich soil and wildflowers.

Patches of trees sparked vivid memories from my childhood. My brothers and I spent many afternoons there, wasting away time and sharing the water of whomever had any left. We'd hide in the shade for hours when our father had told us we couldn't come back in until our chores were complete. A worn down wooden structure showed its head after a few silent minutes of riding. The tree house James had tried to build for me ages ago when I'd begged for one for my tenth birthday.

Seth's tan, freckled face beamed with the joy and freedom that riding brought him. He looked at Hunter, exchanging the silent words that only twins could do. The stormy blue eyes we all shared glimmered as they fell on me with a wicked grin. "Hold on tight."

With a series of gleeful whoops and shouts, the wind ripped in my ears as my brothers took off. Daisy's and Freedom's tails trailed behind them like banners, their feet moving so fast, I could not decipher when they were touching the ground. Freedom and Seth moved as one, the two of them in their element.

I loosened the grip I had on Hunter, my arms out wide, thighs tightened for stability. My laughter mingling with the wind as we raced across the open field. The pressure and expectations our daddy had on us felt far away out here. Understanding why my brothers spent so much time away and out on the property was easy with this kind of reminder. In sync, Hunter and Seth slowed to a steady trot. They rode side by side, the only sounds now the soft clop of hooves and the buzz of nature around us.

Hunter was the first to break the silence. "Anything from that school yet? SCAT?"

"SCAD," Seth corrected, noting the sharp dart of my eyes on the ground and failure to answer the question. He moved Freedom closer, peering at me from beneath his favorite pinched front cowboy hat. "Don't sweat it. Their loss."

The words meant a heck of a lot coming from him. He'd been the main one crapping on the idea of leaving this place along with our dad. "I never applied."

"What?" Hunter asked, turning slightly to get a good look at me. Though he and Seth were twins, they were opposites despite the even amount of time spent in the sun. His pale skin and dark hair resisted the changes from the harsh sun, much like my own. "Why? You were so excited."

"Dad ... he didn't think it was a smart move. A waste of money," I answered, more meekly than I'd intended. It was a touchy subject, considering there was a chance Seth would somehow find a way to defend the harsh words of our dad. They both intended well, had my best interest at heart, but their words could use a lesson in bedside manner from our momma.

"Since when has dad's opinion meant anything to you?" Hunter's olive-hued skin reddened in frustration.

"I mean, I don't know," I reasoned, tucking a loose strand of hair behind my ear. "He's right. I'm of better use out here, anyway. If I leave, y'all would need to hire a ranch hand. We can't afford that and school. Makes sense. I get it. Honest."

"Fuck that, Reina, and fuck what happens here. You deserve to go," Hunter snarled. He was the more protective of my brothers. Always looking out for me, considering my wants and needs. They tended to come last in this house, whether it was intentional or not. Not with Hunter, though. He always put me first. It was admirable —his selflessness. If more people could have a heart as golden as his, then one day the world would be a better place for it.

"Hunter," Seth warned.

"We can pick up the slack around here," Hunter said

definitively. The defiance in his ice-blue stare left Seth little room to argue. With a deep sigh, Seth nodded in agreement. "The two of us will talk to dad."

"Yeah. You just focus on getting in. Go sew a new top for your application or something."

I smiled at Seth. If he'd allow it, I'd smother him with a hug. He tried to understand my world, he really did, and I could only love him for it. "That's not how that works." I looked between the two of them, waiting for them to say sike. "Really though. Y'all sure? No take backs."

"Yeah, we're sure. You let us handle—" Hunter's sentence cut off at the sudden God-awful alarm blaring from his phone. He raised his hips a bit, pulling it loose from his pocket. His fingers trembled as I fought to make out the words on his screen, to no avail.

Buzzing tickled the butt of my pants, the silent mode of my phone saving my heart from another scare. I freed it from the back pocket of my jeans and nearly dropped it at the header of the news alert. Daisy huffed, her movements becoming jerky from the anxiety flowing from my brother and me.

"What?" Seth asked. "What happened? Ma okay?"

He never took his phone when he left the house. Technology and him weren't exactly two peas in a pod and he preferred the peace that came with the disconnection on a ride away from home.

"We need to get home. Now." Hunter nudged Daisy, and she took off at full-speed. The urgency in her gait was eerie. Like she knew the world was ending.

Tacos and Terror

RILEY

I screwed up.

Taking London to a market full of options was going to make it impossible to drag her away before her curfew. Five p.m. sharp. I found it rather unreasonable. I was her brother—there wasn't a thing that could happen to her with me around.

"Oh. My. God. Try this," London said, her twists smacking against my chest as she spun around.

The strong scent of pepper hit me a second before the sweet yet savory cheese melted in my mouth. I arched a brow. "Not bad. Would have been better if I fed it to myself."

"Now with the jam," she ordered, holding out the next piece for me to grab.

I took it begrudgingly, if for no other reason than to

speed up our never ending tour of the Ferry Building Marketplace. To be fair, it was phenomenal. Hell of a lot better than the Kraft I slammed on pieces of bread or instant ramen I called dinner seven days a week. My sister's wide brown eyes stared at me, awaiting a reaction.

"Delicious." I smiled, wrapping an arm around her shoulder and guiding her away.

"Look! Handmade soaps."

London wiggled away from me and made a straight shot for a booth a few spots down. I followed behind her, crumbling the few dollars I had left inside my pocket. She took a deep breath and closed her eyes. "These smell amazing, Riley. Maybe if you get some, you can find yourself a girlfriend."

Tugging her from the soaps with a nod toward the vendor, I steered her in the direction of what we'd come here for—street tacos and chicharrones. I damn near drooled at the smell. The scent of sizzling meat and corn tortillas wafted through the air. Weaving through the crowd, we dodged a couple taking selfies and swerved around a dad trying to soothe his toddler from a full meltdown.

The taco cart wasn't the most popular in the marketplace, but that's what we preferred. Hidden gems were often the most worthy of your time. Gia, the vendor's daughter, waved me over as she saw our approach. Her dad, Jorge, offered a wide smile, his stained apron coated in spices and oil from working the grill. He slid our usual over to Gia with a slight nod before turning back to flip over the tortillas.

"This one's on us, our favorite customers," Gia said, though the pity in her eyes led me to believe it was a far more gracious extension than favoritism.

"Thanks, Gi." London eagerly grabbed the trays of food from her, not giving me the chance to offer up any cash. "Keep it in your pockets, Ril. A gift is a gift."

We found two seats on a bench near the entrance. Balancing the plate on my knees, I ate half the taco in one bite. It was damn good. 'Dreaming about it for the last week' kind of good. London froze as she took her first bite. I followed her eye-line, noticing the group of girls laughing a few feet over.

"You good?" I asked.

"Yeah. This has been fun," she said, tearing her eyes away and taking a minute to chew her food. "Wish we could do this more often. I mean, I guess we can once the judge makes their decision."

I stuffed the rest of the taco in my mouth, buying myself some time. You would think keeping siblings together would be a first priority to the state. The group of girls passed by, glaring down at my sister. London held her stare, her head following them as they made their exit.

"The hell was that about?"

"Nothing I can't handle on my own," she replied, standing up to toss her tray. Her posture had stiffened, though she shrugged off the interaction. "Just some girls from school."

Pushing to my feet, I slapped a hand across the top of her back. "Wouldn't doubt it. Italian ice for the road?"

London went back to the bench for our chicharrones, a large grin taking over her worried features. "Obviously. I'll wait here." She took a seat, popping open the bag and dropping a chip into her mouth.

Shaking my locs, I bunched them into a band to keep the heat off my neck. The nerves were getting to me. The truth of our situation should have been the first thing I'd started our day with. But I knew my sister. London would have spent every second we had together today trying to find a solution to our problem that wasn't hers to solve. It was mine. I pivoted on my heels, turning back to tell her our permanent reality. A high-pitched scream sounded to my left. The synchrony of alarms bellowed from the phones of every person around me.

Mass panic ensued. The screams and cries of terror blended together, making it impossible to decipher the source. I fumbled around for my phone, finding it in my front pocket only to see it had died. *Shit, London.* Thoughts scrambled, I searched for my sister through the sea of bodies. She stood atop the bench we'd eaten at only minutes before. Her deep brown skin was ashen. My sister's eyes stayed locked on her phone as she did her best to avoid the surrounding stampede.

Shoving through the crowd, I made my way to her and scooped her into my arms. Her phone fell from her hands, a muffled, exhausted sob croaked from her throat.

"London?" I kept pace with the herd. Concern was

not an acceptable description to match how I felt. She didn't answer me, only kept her blank stare down at her hands. I couldn't carry her this way, not forever.

Taking a quick survey of the world around us, I found a corner absent from chaos and set her down. Her knees buckled, unable to support her weight. "London!" I shook her, desperate for her to snap back to the present.

She turned her head ever so slightly, dread filling her gaze. "It's over. We're fucked."

Peaceful Silence

TOMOE

The peace that came from utter silence was equivalent to a hand full of gold. Silence in Colorado woods, however, was never good. There were answers in silence. As peaceful as it was, it was unnatural for the world to go mute. If it did, one should listen.

Fresh air was good for the soul but could harm the mind. The stillness and quiet of complete solitude, it played tricks that were dangerous, made you drop your guard. Put you at ease when you should listen to the gentle warning of mother nature and all she has to offer. Silence ironically presented both peace and danger. Though the two could exist at once, I knew we were not the only apex predator in these woods. Lair o' the Bear Park was full of wildlife—some of which I'd be more delighted to run into than others.

"June," I said, reaching a hand out to halt my sister at my side.

She looked down at my hand, then up at me with an expecting stare. I motioned for her to remove her earphones, and she rolled her eyes. A heavy sigh preceded her impatient rounds of questions. "Yes, Tomoe? Can I help you? What is the point of a mindful walk if you're going to stop and interrupt us every few feet?"

"It's quiet again," I leveled, peering over my shoulder. "And take your headphones off. Don't be an idiot."

"Oh lighten up, it's ocean sounds. I can still hear. Also, you made the tea too strong." The dark freckles around her nose bunched in a display of disgust.

I took it from her, downing what was left with a straight face, then handed her back the tumbler. "We should go back."

"If we turned around every time you got a gut feeling, we would have never made it out of the parking lot."

June kept walking, her silky bob swishing with the cool breeze. Scanning the dense forests and the swiftly moving creek slithering beside us, I let another moment pass, then jogged up behind her. Still, the skin on the back of my neck prickled with fear. The sound of my sister's voice trickled around the bend of the trail, followed by the flirtatious laugh she released when she was flustered.

"Just followed you back," she swooned visibly, passing the phone back to one of the two men up ahead. June toyed with her shorts, changing her stance to make her hip pop out to the side as she ruffled back her hair to add volume.

The tallest of the two chuckled. "I'll DM you. Nice to meet you, June," he called over his shoulder.

Both of them nodded at me as they passed, the second one offering me a cocky smirk. "What's up?"

I rolled my eyes, making my way toward my sister, then thought better of it. Warning them was the least I could do. One human to the next or whatever. "Careful down there. Woods are quiet," I said, turning around to face them.

The shorter, blond one shook a canister of bear spray above his head, not bothering to glance back. "We're covered. Thanks. Enjoy the hike!"

June kept her eyes on her prize, peering behind me to take in all of him. I nudged her to keep going. She bit her lip, refusing to move. I couldn't help myself. I burst into a fit of laughter. The girl was easily distracted by anything that could flash a decent smile, and I loved her for it. Between her and our other sister, Kana, they kept that little light going in my life. Someone had to be the serious one of the bunch though, and I happily fulfilled that role. But the universe demanded balance. It was nice to get a good laugh every now and then.

I reared behind her, pushing her to keep going. "Come on. Let's go."

"What?" she said, finally closing her dropped jaw. "He was cute."

"No. He was just tall with dark eyes in a $400 Patagonia jacket."

June shrugged. "Same thing."

We continued in silence along the trail. The towering pines and soothing trickle of water soothing a piece of my soul. It wasn't so quiet with the creek flowing and the whispering of trees in the wind.

The tranquility of the trail was shattered. A startled scream echoed by an agonizing holler bounced off the trees. I held my breath, listening for what was sure to follow. The cry of a mountain lion was unmistakable. If you heard it once, you would never forget it. Whatever screeched into the stark silent air next was neither human nor animal.

In times of fear, I found there were two reactions that sealed one's fate. The ability to think clearly, and the hesitancy to respond. One was damning, the other was not. We reached for our phones at the same time. There was nothing we could do for them besides call for help. Even with bear spray and a taser, it would be inadequate to whatever had caused that soul-breaching of a scream.

Paralyzed. The bone-chilling alert on the screen of my phone was paralyzing. "June ..."

"Yeah?" She trembled in response.

I looked up, shock etched on her face as the pale of her skin turned a ghostly white. "Help isn't coming anytime soon."

"Yeah." June mumbled. "Agreed."

We stood frozen in place, the earthy scent of the forest

bringing me a sense of calm. Grounding me in place. June's breaths mirrored mine, shallow and uneven. Her dark eyes narrowed and then widened, stuck in an infinite loop between her phone to the shadows lurking in the trees. I didn't need to know what my little sister was thinking. The panic she was talking herself down from. Our minds were racing, yet no clear plan of action found us. The trail we had walked down so many times now felt like a maze of uncertain doom and hidden dangers.

"What do we do?" June asked, her voice barely an octave above a whisper.

I tugged on my sleeves, nails digging into my palms. "We need to move. Staying put is dumb. We're sitting ducks. Let's go."

Go. Speaking the word was humorous. Go where? Move where? We needed to get out of here. I knew that much. But the rest ... the future ... that had suddenly become an open-ended question.

Hellbent

Alexiares

Every time I closed my eyes at night, I worried how much of my humanity remained. In each passing day, the monster I pretended to be, that everyone thought I was, no longer could be claimed as an act. I got it now. *The darkest hour never comes in the night.*

A funeral. How fucking fitting that this all started after the celebration of the end of a life. I want to take a moment here to highlight the deliberate use of the word.

Throbbing, pulsating, shots of pain radiated through my skull, the loud roar of the Kawasaki humming between my legs. That's what I got for getting absolutely hammered the night before such an event. For once in my miserable existence, I wished I had been on time so I could have caught a ride with my parents—no matter how insufferable sitting in the car with my father was.

Anything was better than the grinding that came from this souped-up baby I'd worked on during the sleepless nights, Alexander Drakos in mind. He hated the attention it brought. The neighbors didn't look our way much ... until they did. It wasn't as if they didn't know we were there. Journalists sat outside our gates like vultures, and my sweet ride signaled to everyone within a few miles that I was headed home.

I didn't regret shit, but in this decision, I may have a passing thought or two of 'What if you weren't such a spiteful dick?'

The slight sensation of vibrations teased against my thigh. Then another. *Shit*, my phone was blowing up. I leaned to my right, taking my left hand off the handle to pull it out and see what all the commotion was about. If the truth came out about the deal I screwed up for my old man on today of all days, it may very well be my funeral my mother arranged next.

A glimmer of water caught my eye, the bridge not too far ahead. I righted my position. We were only a few minutes off from the house. Whatever was going on would still be a crisis when we arrived. With my mom right behind me, it wasn't worth the fuss, anyway.

She hated the bike, was uncomfortable with the 'risk' I took driving it all the time. I didn't have the heart to tell her that the risk brought me the only sense of freedom I'd ever felt in my life. Driving with one hand, on a motorcycle, over the bridge, while reading whatever was on my phone, would give her a fucking aneurysm.

The smell of burning rubber filtered into my helmet. A distant, imperceptible sound stiffened the bones beneath my skin. I ignored it, shaking it off as an adrenaline rush from riding in the rain. This bridge was slippery as hell when wet.

Everyone that lived on the other side enjoyed the natural privacy the instability of the bridge brought on rainy days. The undeniable, ear-ringing screech of tires shot my heart into the depths of my stomach. I glanced ahead, checking to make sure the road laid out before me was clear before whipping my head around. The blacked out Suburban my parents and my little brother Evander were being escorted in swerved out of control as it sped through the entrance of the bridge.

I slid into a U-turn, the water building on the bridge splashed into my boots as I let my foot guide the bike around safely. The SUV jerked back and forth, like someone was fighting to right the path it was flying down. A car sped from behind them, attempting to get ahead of the crash. It clipped me as I swerved around them, sending me from the bike, as it collided with their front end and slid into the windshield.

Rolling against the asphalt, my skin burned, the thin sleeves of my suit jacket not enough against the speed I'd fallen at. Crunching metal sang through the crisp Illinois air. The world stopped spinning. Dust settled. The result of the crash revealed itself.

My parents' SUV rested atop the Ford Fiesta beneath them, the only thing supporting them from toppling over the bridge. There was no one in the car. The driver's window was broken, blood sprayed about the tan cloth seats. *Holy fucking ...*

Muffled, panicked shouts for help sounded from inside the SUV. I raced over, throwing open the back seat door of the Fiesta and locking the tip of my boots beneath the seat. I latched on to the 'oh shit handle' above the window of the car for support.

The driver in the front slammed back and forth in his seat, stuck behind his seat belt. *Who would've thought, Mr. Fiesta, that a seat belt could save your life?* He could recover from a seizure. I just had to figure out how to get them all out the car. Taking a look around, I made note of everyone's condition. Evander and my mother seemed to be in shock but overall okay, my father on the other hand, lay knocked out against the window. Blood dripped from under his dark brows, his lips twitching.

I met Evander's deep green eyes dilated fear. He clutched onto the back of my mom's chair. His raven colored hair was clumped with blood on the sides. No signs of pain registered in the ghostly gaze staring back at me.

"Get him out, Alexi, please!"

Her cries centered me, forcing me to focus on the imminent danger of the situation.

Releasing my hold on the inside of the Fiesta, I reached into the Suburban slowly, careful not to redistribute too much of my weight.

"Evander," I said, doing my best to keep the fear from my voice. "Grab onto my hand. Keep your movements slow, down the center of the aisle from the back then stop. When I give you the go, make yourself loose, I'll pull you out. Got it?"

He nodded, jaw clenched, his olive skin a muted green. At sixteen, he was almost my height. This was going to be tricky since getting all the way in the back of that thing was an uncomfortable task for us under normal circumstances. Evander kept his eyes on me, following my instructions down to the detail, hitting the ground with a grunt.

Our father came to, the sound of Evander gasping for air forced him to confront the here and now. He glanced out the window, not liking his odds if this thing went over. Scrambling for the exit, the movements shook both cars.

"Chill the fuck out or you'll going to kill us all," I raised my voice over the chaos unfolding around me.

Evander clawed the ground behind me in utter despair. None of my words registered. The only thing consuming his thoughts was the danger that lurked on the other side of the car.

I scanned the scene, trying to come up with a way to get them both out before our time and luck ran out. Securing my feet in the Fiesta, I shifted my weight back, yelling for Evander to snap out of it and provide support from behind.

Releasing my grip again, I reached back into the car. "Mom. Same as Evander. Move slowly and lock your hand in mine." I met my father's panic stricken stare, doing my best to calm the man who never let me show a single emotion in my life. *Now look at him, pathetic.* "When I say go, Evander is going to support my weight, I'll pull mom out, in that same motion, you grab onto my other hand."

I knew the plan sucked. I'm not even sure I expected it to work, but it was all I had. One look around and I could see that not only was no help on the way, there wasn't a single soul outside of my family in sight. So I rolled with what I had.

"Get me out of here, you *worthless boy*," my father snarled, as if he were in the position to make demands.

Yes, sir.

My mom's forest green eyes shimmered with tears, her small, clammy palm clasping within mine. "I got you, sweetie. I'm ready."

"Evander, let's go," I said, putting all my trust in him.

The car wobbled, fear coursing through my father's veins. He pounced, latching on to my mom's curly brown hair and taking hold of my free hand. She screeched, the sensation taking her by surprise. Her hand left mine.

I lunged forward to hell with him. He fell back onto the window as I let go of his hold, trying to secure my connection back into my mom's. Our fingers brushed against each other, but it was too late.

The only thing keeping me from falling with them

was Evander's hold of my shirt. Gravity failed me as I flailed backward, landing atop Evander, a whoosh of air leaving his lungs.

Time is not linear.

The future and the past blurred. Time slowed. I didn't even hear the splash as the SUV sent my parents tumbling to imminent death.

The man who caused so much death had been scared of dying. How poetic. I hope he burned in hell for an eternity.

I rolled myself off Evander, laying on my back and staring up at the darkening sky. He wheezed, breaths sounding painful as they escaped his lips. I placed my hand on his chest, pressing around to make sure nothing was broken. Too much energy. It would take too much energy to push myself up.

The buzzing had stopped. *How odd.* Calling for help hadn't even occurred to me now. What help was I calling for?

There was no one left to save.

"No signal," Evander huffed, shoving his phone into my face.

I grabbed onto it, doing a double take, not recalling him getting up. His back was rigid as he stared at the side of the bridge, the Ford Fiesta the only vehicle remaining.

"You need help?" I asked, taking note of his hand resting on his rib cage.

"Been through worse."

In a swift movement, I pressed to my feet, offering him a hand. He took it though his stubborn nature kept his eyes from leaving the last place we'd seen our parents alive.

I checked my phone, blood chilling the flesh around my bones. "No bars."

The recollection of the buzzing nauseated the inner part of my ear as the world around me filled with white stars. Each notification cluttering up my home screen was worse than the last. The ground beneath me swirled as if I'd had five shots too many.

"They pushed the big red button," I said. "Let's go."

"What button? Go where?" Evander asked, his voice distant, detached.

He sounded his age. Something I'd never heard him sound like before. I had to remind myself constantly that my brother was only sixteen. With everything he had seen, heard ... been through, it was easy to forget.

I didn't answer him.

Home.

It was the only place we could go. There was nothing left for us on this bridge. No one was coming. No one would ever come, not for a long-ass time.

It was just us now. There was no changing that. I waited for the tears to fall, but none came. No sadness filled my heart, only anger soothed my soul.

Hellbent.

I was hellbent my entire life on destroying everything my father touched. To be the opposite of him was to be a better man. Now the word had a different definition. A different intention. *Hellbent.* To keep my brother alive, I would become the man we both feared.

Part Two
THE GENERAL

THE END

AMAIA

This is the end. It has to be. Please let it be.

The world did not end with an asteroid, or climate change, or super volcano. No. No one considered that the world would be brought to its knees by an unfathomable scenario.

Society did not crumble, one empire after another. Humanity destroyed each other, yes. But the world I now lived in, the world I was forced to survive, I don't suppose an author or screenwriter could properly depict it even if they tried.

Hell. Chaos. Death.

So much death.

That about summed it up. Death lingered in the air, complementing the permanent stench of rotten eggs and the taste of metal coating my tongue. I was foolish to have left without my gas mask, grabbing my bug-out bag in such a hurry. I had been careless and arrogant in ignoring my dad's insistence on keeping my mask in the bag for this exact situation. Okay, maybe not *exact*.

My mom and I had teased him relentlessly about his doomsday prepper hobby, insisting that years in the military had muddled his brain. A career based on preparing for the worst, most inconceivable situations could do that to a person. Joke was on me, I guess.

A tear dripped down my face at the thought of never being able to tell him he was right, the opportunity gone along with my parents. Only hours ago, the cell towers had connected for a brief moment. Long enough for my best friend Sammy to get through to her family and check in, while I impatiently tried to reach my own. The line didn't even connect. In truth, I knew they were gone. There had been a sense of finality in my father's last text. No texts from Sloan popped up and mine hadn't delivered. And then Sammy was gone too.

At least she got to say goodbye. The door behind me thudded against my skull, the impact catching me off guard. A deep growl hummed near my feet. Harley's tail tucked and ears flattened against her head.

"Shh, it's okay, girl. It's okay," I cooed, crouching down to rub her silky black fur. My hands shook in unison with the door behind me, a series of groans and guttural screeches finding their way beneath the door.

I just needed a second to think. Put together a plan. Lack of planning put me in this situation to begin with.

The smart thing would have been to head back to my apartment on day one with Sammy in tow. It would have been safer, and there would have been a better chance of making it to the storage unit on the other side of town alive. Probably would have been easier to stock up on ammo and weapons the first day too.

Hindsight's 20/20, and I had been too weak to make my move then, anyway.

And now, I was out of options and forced to face my new reality. The key I needed to retrieve my own weapons was behind the door I leaned against, my mask too. I wouldn't be able to make it across town and to wherever was next without them. My dead slash undead fiancé slammed his body against it. *You could try a gun store.* But chances were, there was nothing left worth risking my life. Especially unarmed.

Fuck it, I thought as I rammed against the now unlocked door. There was no plan that would get me what I needed. I had no weapons other than one of the hunting knives from my bag, and our studio apartment left little to no room for improvising. My best chance would be to bum-rush past him and try to maneuver my way back out. I had the speed, and if I had to, I could fight my way out. I'd always been able to hold my own. My dad had made sure of it.

I rammed the door open hard enough that Xavier was thrown into the wall. The stun of the impact bought me half a second before he lunged, narrowly missing my body as I fell onto my back, scrambling to get upright again.

Frantically, I searched for my knife now tossed somewhere around the room.

My fingers grazed sand scattered on the floor from the shattered hermit crab tank. Xavier was on the ground now, on all fours, dragging himself near me, jaw slack. *Broken,* I realized. Probably from the thud against the door. He looked worse from the last time I'd laid eyes on him. Left him. Abandoned him like the awful person I realized I was becoming. His once warm, brown skin was now ashen and visibly clammy. His eyes, empty.

A yelp escaped my throat as Harley closed in. "No!"

I reached for her, not wanting her to be in harm's way as sand rose through the air, hovering for just a moment before flinging toward Xavier's neck and face. The movement so swift, I nearly missed the crystallized fragments that entered his body. Dark brown blood oozed from his wounds, the pain not registering as his jaw clattered at an unnatural angel, still reaching to connect with my skin.

In the grip of panic, my feet refused to lie flat against the floor, trying to process how I had done that. *If* I had done it. He lunged again, this time connecting with my shoe. The thick sole of my boots prevented his teeth from piercing my skin. Harley whimpered, not sure what to do or how to protect me, bringing his attention back to her.

I rolled to my knees, kicking my feet free, ready to place myself between them. My hands burned, breaking my focus momentarily. *Ow. What? Shit.* I shook my hands as flames kissed the palm of my hand. It wasn't burning me, but the heat of the flames had startled me enough for me to want them gone. Unsure how to put them out, I grimaced as I placed them against Xavier's shoulders. I didn't want to hurt him—merely wanted to push him back and away from us both. They went out before we touched.

Time froze. Xavier glanced down at his body, pausing as if registering that he was not on fire. I took advantage, using the precious seconds to leap toward the junk drawer in the kitchen's island. Eyeing Xavier stumbling and failing to get to his feet, I rumbled around, tossing items out in search of the key. *Got it.* Something bumped into my calf, drawing my gaze down. Harley backed into my leg, body tense and ready to protect.

Xavier dragged himself across the floor, closing in inch by inch as I backed against the wall, ready to grab Harley and leap over him. She dodged my grasp, circling Xavier and barely missing his reach.

"Please," I begged them both. "Please stop. Harley, come here, girl. Come to momma." She ignored me, her snarl threatening. Warning him not to get closer. One blink and Xavier's teeth were latched onto Harley's hide. An agonizing yelp of pain filled the air. My body covered hers in an instant. A heavy, throbbing sensation shot through the back of my leg. I didn't need to look back to know what happened.

Using my body weight, I tossed my free leg away from my body, thrusting my arm back and forcing him beneath me. Straddling his waist, I reached for my knife on the ground. Harley limped to my side, relentless in her attempt to keep me safe. I searched the hollow, empty eyes beneath me, trying to find any piece of the man I had loved trapped inside.

I'd been holed up in Sammy's apartment for a week. The only up close and personal encounter with the undead being Xavier and the elderly couple who had grabbed Sammy on our way out hours ago.

Before this, I'd often wondered if my life was threatened, or the people I'd loved were at risk, if I'd choose fight or flight. Everybody wants to be the badass. Imagines themselves the hero. The person who'd save the day and be fearless. Shit, I thought that would've been me.

Flight had won out each time.

Xavier wiggled under me. His arms flailing around, trying to find something to take hold of to free himself. Clammy fingers found themselves rooted in my scalp, weaving their way through my curls and yanking my head back.

"Xavier, stop. Listen to me, it's me! My love, I need you to hear my voice. Focus," I said, pleading with him to fight whatever sickness this was.

His grip tightened, pulling my body up enough to find leeway, his jaw clenching around my wrist and drawing back. The pain seared, forcing me back forward to keep him from tearing away my skin.

"Baby, please," I begged. His only response was to bite harder.

My knife entered his chest. No relief. I pulled it free, driving it in again. Nothing. No sign of him feeling a thing, no grumble of pain or sign of weakening. *No. No, you can't.* Another dive into his torso. Hollywood had a habit of getting things wrong for the sake of cinema, but something told me they had gotten this one thing right. Desensitizing us to what would eventually come to fruition.

"I love you, Xavier. I love you forever," I choked out, tears streaming down my face.

I drove my blade into his skull and his body went limp beneath me.

Time sped back up. Hours passed; Harley lay in my lap as I sat leaned against the island cabinets. My body trembled. *Did I kill him? Oh God, he was still in there. He thought I burned him; he could feel pain. I killed him. I'm a murderer. I killed him. I'm a killer.*

Xavier's body sat a few feet away, unmoving and lifeless, as the last two years of our life together passed through my mind. The late nights talking in bed, planning our future. Double dates with friends, creating new holiday traditions of our own, saving for our first house together.

All of it for nothing.

He had died a week ago, and I would die next to his body today. I rocked Harley back and forth, waiting for time to claim us and the disease to take hold. There was no panic. I wasn't sure if animals could turn, but if she did, once she did, I'd keep myself from hurting the next person. Take myself out of the equation. There was no need for another threat to be unleashed into this world, ruining someone else's chance at whatever future remained. I'd seen all the movies and shows. I knew how infections worked, how they spread. I'd put an end to it right here.

"I'm sorry, Harley girl. This wasn't how I imagined we'd meet our end, but at least we're all going together."

My eyes opened; daylight streamed in through the smog-filled sky. Awakening back in my apartment was strange after a week away, but Xavier's body cleared up any confusion the morning had brought. I shook Harley, making sure she was still with me as she startled awake. Her hind leg gave out from muscle tension around her wound, but she was alive.

My eyes shot to my leg and wrist next. On the verge of infection, but my consciousness was still in place. Pushing to my feet, I limped over to the bathroom, stepping over the fragments of the door to stare at myself in the mirror. Curls were strewn in every direction. My bun was now a small cluster held in place with a scrunchie, a bald spot on the side from Xavier's grip. But my face was normal. Red scratches littered my cheeks and jaw. Blood had dripped down my now torn pants onto my brown skin, but I wasn't infected.

At least not yet.

I wouldn't let myself harbor on that, setting into motion and grabbing a bottle of ninety-eight proof alcohol off the bar cart near the door. Sammy and I used it for party punch. My hands shook at the thought of how we'd never do that together again as I brought Harley's bed toward her, motioning for her to lie down.

"This is gonna hurt, but it's okay. I'm here with you," I said, rubbing her to calm her down. I poured the liquor on the wound, not giving her time to react as I pulled a treat off the edge of the table, offering her immediate gratification.

Pulling my pants down, I grabbed Xavier's work belt off the chair he'd grown accustomed to using to store random items of clothing at the end of a long day. Grimacing, ready for the pain, I placed it between my teeth. "My turn next."

Grunting at the ironically relieving pain, I moved on to my wrist, patting both areas dry before dropping to pull a bandage from my bag. Wrapping Harley's wounds, then my own, I pulled on another pair of cargos from my closet and grabbed my gas mask from the corner.

Placing the storage key in my pocket, I cloaked Xavier in the throw blanket from the couch, kissing the top of his head. "Goodbye, my love. I'll find you in the next life and whatever comes after that."

Taking a swig from the bottle I'd used to treat our wounds, I double checked my mental list. It could be the difference between life and death if I left prematurely, only to find out I needed to grab something else I would need out on the road. I'd packed whatever dog food, medication, and canned goods I could carry into the remaining space in my bag and then placed Harley's leash around her harness.

I took one last look around the room, what had been my home, *our home.*

"Harley girl," I said, "This is going to fucking suck. No, screw that, it's going to hurt like hell to get there, and I don't even know where there is. But this isn't our end. Nope, our story has just begun."

Run Girl, Run

AMAIA

ACROSS THE ROOM, A PHONE RANG. A SOUND I hadn't heard in a week, a sound I never thought I'd hear again. It wasn't mine. That wasn't my ringtone. Light brown hair whipped around as golden eyes met my own. It was Sammy's.

"Answer it," I said, springing her into action as the shock wore off.

The book she'd been reading fell off her lap, the thud waking Harley from a deep sleep. Both of us watched Sammy answer cautiously.

"Hello," her voice trembled. "Mom?"

The scene changed. Sammy faced me, an eager look on her face as she tried to contain her excitement for my sake. She hadn't asked, hadn't needed to, to know that there was no word from Sloan and my family was gone. That I didn't *have a refuge the way she did; I no longer had a home to go back to. Not an apartment. Not to my parents. Just her and Harley.*

"Ready?" she asked, pulling her keys from her pocket, ready to lock the door for a reason we weren't quite sure of.

If someone really wanted to get in, they could. We had no idea what life had turned into outside the walls and the safety of the place we'd hidden in. Simpletons, waiting for news about the state of our country or any plans to recover from this mess. We could see a sliver of the main street from her apartment window, but it wasn't pretty. Few people wandered out on the street and the ones that did ... well, we often heard them screaming shortly after. Whether it was people or those things outside, we weren't sure and we defi-nitely weren't trying to find out.

Sammy never saw them coming, but I did. They were fast. Too fast for the elderly couple we had known through the few years she had lived here. The same sweet old couple who had asked us to keep it down late nights. Bribing our silence with leftovers, an attempt to put us into a food induced coma. I'd spent many weekends away from school, coming back to check on my best friend.

One second she was next to me, ready to see what the world had left to offer us. Smiling. Hopeful. Alive. And then she was gone. Her arms swinging wildly, trying to fight off what she couldn't see. The shape of an 'O' formed on her lips, but no scream left. Her eyes were wide, searching mine for answers.

For help.

Help I could not offer, as their teeth broke the skin of her shoulders and then her neck. Blood splattered against the wall; warm, metallic scented drops flecked against my cheek. Horror rooted me in place, and I waited for my brain to catch up and decide what to do.

The elderly man tore from her shoulder, moving up and latching onto her cheek. Her eyes, the only visible part of her face. I fumbled in my bag for a weapon—anything that I could use—remembering the hunting knives I'd buried at the bottom. The movement drew the attention of the elderly woman, her eyes curiously glancing over me for half a second.

I ran.

My eyes opened, sweat covering my body, stomach clenching. That wasn't a nightmare, but rather a haunting memory—one I deserved to have for the rest of my life. I rolled over, bile rising in my throat and finding freedom in the industrial carpet beneath me. Wiping the corners of my mouth, I pulled myself up to the edge of the windowsill. I raised a pair of binoculars to my face, scanning the town below as I had for the past twenty-four hours.

Going through a city was my least favorite activity, but I was low on food and the small town outside Salem, Oregon, beckoned me with the promise of finding some. Alcohol lined my stomach more than food did. For some reason, it was easier to come by than an old can of vegetables. That was fine. I could get by on less, but Harley couldn't. Half of the food I gathered went to her. Hunting was an option, but wasting that energy to not eat the meat myself seemed like an unnecessary effort.

I laughed to myself, thinking of how my father would make a snide remark about the end of the world, and I still let my conscience control my eating habits. Driving a knife through a human skull, no problem. But actively hunting and preparing the meat of an animal capable of forming complex thoughts? Absolutely not. So canned food and a distilled beverage it was. Harley wasn't picky and caught enough small game to sustain herself more times than not.

My own health didn't matter. I no longer cared about myself. Simply wanted to make sure Harley lived. She was all I had left. I'd never considered myself a materialistic person, but damn, did I miss my things. My books, cozy blankets, my coffee machine. *Oh, to have a cup of coffee.* My mouth watered. Music. I hadn't expected to miss music or even TV Most of my free time was spent reading, and if I wasn't reading, I was listening to an audiobook in the car, in the shower, or as I cleaned.

Sushi, good lord I missed sushi. I missed my life, my friends. *Sloan,* I wondered, letting my mind drift to my friend from university. Flame encased my body as my thoughts drifted toward the people I knew were gone. People I'd have to miss forever. My parents. Xavier. Sammy. The latter two losses would be a source of self-hatred for the rest of my life. My own inaction being the reason they'd never live another day.

Only one life depended on me now, and I'd be damn sure to keep her alive. The fire surrounding me died down under focus. Several buildings had succumbed to my flames in the process of figuring out my triggers and I still didn't have them completely under control.

What happened after the bombs went off two months ago wasn't clear. I didn't travel in groups. Any information I'd come by had been limited, knowledge gained from spying or hiding and overhearing. Three things were clear, however. I wasn't alone. You could be gifted with things other than fire, and if you were lucky the way I was, you could have the gift of more than one.

But there were also people who weren't lucky. I'd observed them from afar and studied them up close, but there hadn't been any outward similarities. No one else had determined a cause for their demise, either.

It wasn't a transferable disease. Their bites wouldn't cause you to be infected, though they hurt like hell. *Pansies*, I'd heard a few groups call them. No rhyme or reason to it, someone had mentioned. A name that had stuck.

To me, it just felt fitting. They were fast and strong, but their bones were frail—easy to pierce—and their movements wild and uncoordinated.

I gathered our belongings, confident in my decision to leave after not having seen much movement throughout the streets over the last day. There were a few Pansies straggling around, but nothing we couldn't dodge. We'd finessed our way through far worse these past few months.

Five minutes later, I was forced to swallow my words. Sticking to the sides of the buildings and keeping my eyes up and around, a small cluster of Pansies from inside the windowless storefront escaped my radar. Harley barked in alarm. A hand closed in on her tail, dragging her toward the broken glass and inside the building.

Huffing a sigh, I drew my knife from the holster at my hip. A physical fight was exactly what I needed to relieve the tension building up beneath my skin. The emotions from my restless sleep craved release. Six quick and efficient movements later, and they were down. The blade of my knife entered their skulls with what would once have been a sickening wet slush. I could have ended them in three, but there was something poetic about even numbers. Smearing their rust-colored blood across my pants, I gave Harley a pat on the head. My eyes scanned the length of her body, checking for injuries but finding none.

Placing my knife back at my side, I removed the glass bottle from my bag. Holding my tongue out, I savored the bitter taste of the last drop as I shook the bottle, making sure none went to waste. A sharp laugh scared the shit out of me. Clearing my throat with little recognition. It was hard to accept this pathetic state. I dropped the bottle, head motioning for Harley to get moving again.

"We've got places to be and food to find, my girl," I

sang out, riding the high of putting two down with little effort. *Music, I need music.* It was tactically stupid, but I didn't care, a false sense of invincibility clouded my judgment.

We made it to the next alleyway before a hand covered my mouth, preventing the next words from flowing and sealing my breath. Harley growled, a few quick warning barks unleashed as she latched onto the culprit's leg.

Cold metal jabbed into my neck as a man whispered into my ear, "Call the dog off, or I'll kill you."

He paused, and I calmed my movements, deciding kicking back toward him wouldn't help my situation. "If I die, she'll kill you," I said, gasping for air.

Strong hands grabbed on my shoulders, twisting me around to face him. I studied him; he was older. His face was kind, but weathered, hair gray and fine lines creasing the skin near catlike eyes. Panic set in as I took in his size, and my flames claimed my fists in defense.

He was over a foot taller than me, the muscle in his build making what was sure to be an extra-large shirt appear as an extra-small. He had either roided up before this, or had been given an edge on survival after. *Probably both.*

In the days I'd spent observing from tall structures in the cities I passed through, I'd noticed an increase in unusually large people. Some you could tell had already been of substantial size before, either naturally or through enhancers. Others were clumsy. Uncoordinated and not used to their now long limbs or what was likely heightened senses if the size of their nose and eyes were any indication of additional mutations.

The advantage had escaped me, keeping me at the five foot two I was before. I fixed my stance, ready to put additional distance between us, as he interrupted. He put his hands up as if offering peace, face grimaced at Harley still clamped onto his skin, awaiting my next command.

"I'm trying to—" he hissed in pain. "I'm trying to save you, child. There's a group of men a few blocks away. They won't be as pleasant as I am."

I scowled at him. "Bullshit."

Shifting my weight, I raised my hand, still wrapped in flame as I peered behind my shoulder toward the street, then back at him. There was sincerity behind his gaze. My gut told me he was telling the truth, at least about the men.

I doused my flames, calling Harley off, a groan following in relief.

"I'm not a fool," I grumbled. "This isn't so much about saving the two of us as it is about saving yourself. My singing was just drawing attention to your location."

His eyes narrowed at my accusation. "I can do both at the same time. It's human nature to work together to survive. Not everyone in this world is out to get you."

"Likely though," I chuckled, voice laced in sarcasm.

The rumble of a motorcycle sounded, followed by the murmur of voices, a rough male voice ordering a group to spread out. The large man extended an arm, pushing us into the shadows as I pulled my gun, finding security in something I'd been trained to use efficiently. With certainty.

He shook his head. "No. It's too loud, the noise will attract the others. More of them than possible for us to take down fighting."

I grinned, ready to test out the next best option—throwing knives. I'd been practicing for some time, finding them easier to control than the unpredictable flames, meeting my target each time. There was little effort on my end and I didn't have anyone to teach me the correct form. Just had to go with what felt right, but it worked. Both palms tightening on the helm of the knives, I took in a deep breath as the motorcycle passed us.

One breath out. A breath in. Another breath out.

The engine of the motorcycle revved, closing back in on our location. I closed my eyes, and the sound stopped as the engine cut off. Another breath in, and my blades flew through the air, entering near his jugular and clearing straight through his neck.

Harley lunged forward, her jaw secured around his wrist as she dragged him toward the alleyway, synchronizing her movements with me, pulling his bike out of view. I froze. The man hadn't moved. Instead, he watched, studying me. An expression of horror filling the kind features of his face.

"You're too young to know violence like this," he whispered. I wasn't even sure he'd known he'd said the words out loud.

I cleared my throat, uncomfortable under his gaze. "Way of the world now. Do what you have to, to survive."

"It shouldn't have to be that way."

Wishful thinking never got anyone far, I'd wanted to say, but was cut off by the sound of voices nearing closer, searching for a friend they'd have to spend forever missing now too. The only difference being, they'd have the opportunity to kill what had ended the life of someone they loved. They'd be rightful to do so. There were moments I'd wish I could myself, but I couldn't. Wasn't strong enough to, or weak enough to. *Whatever.* Instead, I did what I did best.

I ran.

The Beginning

AMAIA

Fifteen months had passed since the bombs had dropped. My twenty-third birthday had come and gone. It was an eerie feeling. The people I'd celebrated with only a year prior would not live to see their own. Would never see what this world had become.

The air had become easy to breathe without a gas mask, no longer squeezing and releasing your lungs with every step. Each day grew warmer than the one prior as we moved further south. It was bearable, nothing that changed the overall ecosystem too much, though the oceans had yet to recover from the algae lost.

Thirteen months ago, I'd blown the cover of my saving grace. A man of virtue and patience, an ill fit for this world, but his presence alone had spared me from my own demise. Our time on the road created a formidable bond. One I had grown to cherish. Value beyond what I'd conceived as possible in the remains of who I'd been before.

I respected him, loved him like family. Appreciated him for opening my eyes to the idea of forgiveness, not only of myself but toward others. He'd recognized the triggers of my power and helped me learn to control it, learning to listen to myself and my body. I was lucky. Most people had just started to figure their gifts out, but I knew what I was capable of now. Was confident in my abilities.

I'd never run again.

Prescott and I had spent time traveling with a few groups for weeks at a time, never sticking around long. It was nice to stay connected with others. No matter how dark minds had gone, there were still good people out there too.

The rumor mill that ran rampant among groups was an added benefit. You'd hear things. Things that made you question whether it was worth sticking around to see how depraved humanity could get. Watching society feed their beast instead of killing it. There were times when I wondered if humanity deserved to survive at all. Some humans ... most of us truly, were not worthy of this next phase of evolution.

Of course, there were moments of hope, as fleeting as they may be. Word had spread of the government setting up survivor camps outside major cities. We hadn't come across any yet. Nonetheless, we'd started heading in the general direction of Los Angeles, wanting to find a home of our own, no longer having the desire to stay moving all the time. There was no security in that.

"How sad," I said, the acrid smell of smoke and burning materials filled my nostrils. "Was on my bucket list before this. Kind of place you'd stop through on a road trip and take pictures, interact with endearing locals. Sucks I'll never get to really take in its beauty."

The city of Monterey was devastated, wrought by fire. Most of the buildings had been reduced to rubble, the smoldering charred remains still emitting smoke. Debris littered the streets, evidence of the people who'd fled either before or during the flames. A haunting reminder of what my gifts could do if I lost control.

It wasn't the first city we'd come across that had succumbed to flames and was likely not the last. Between people who had turned with flammable material in their surroundings and others with gifts similar to my own, fire departments had quickly become too overwhelmed to put them out. The big 'if' being if the fire department had even remained and hadn't scattered immediately, abandoning all hope.

Prescott wasn't seeing it that way. Where hope had long been lost in a city covered in ash, his eyes glittered with it. I studied the tall, red-haired man on the other side of me. Hope filled his eyes, too. He'd joined us halfway through our journey. We'd been traveling with a smaller group through the Redwoods and for some reason, he just seemed to fit. Our makeshift family of two had become a trio.

He understood me. Related to the loss I'd felt since he'd suffered through his own. Jax provided a sense of safety and security I thought unattainable for our reality. The connection between us healed wounds we'd assumed would bleed forever. There was solace in each other's company.

"Don't know what you're talking about," Prescott murmured absentmindedly. "All I see is the perfect place to call home."

When Jax turned his head down to look at me, his meek grin caused my heart to skip a beat. It wasn't simply a matter of him being timelessly attractive, because there was no doubt about that. But there was something more, something deeper that drew me to him. His reassuring smile was a small comfort in the midst of the chaos of our lives.

I groaned, "Here we go. Pres, it's nothing but rubble."

"San Diego put up walls," he said, speaking out into the distance. Jax didn't react. It was news to me, but clearly, they'd been talking. *Their optimism will be the death of them, I swear.* "They're rebuilding," he continued. "Why join someone else's cause when we can start our own? Control our own future, shape history."

Jax chuckled, turning back to face us after focusing on the horizon. His finger rose, accent thick as he pointed toward the distance on the far left. "I'll be damned. It's not population zero after all."

A small cluster of homes stood out in the distance, smoke snaking out the chimneys indicating signs of life.

This wasn't a city that had crumbled, but rather a city of resilience.

"You know the history, don't you? There's no such thing as a coincidence, Amaia. This is a sign." A few steps and Prescott's warm hand placed over my shoulder, encouraging the tension to leave my body.

San Diego had been the first European settlement in the state, setting the forefront for what would become modern day California. Monterey followed in its footsteps. Had already thrived as a political and religious capital in Mexican California. After Mexico had ceded the state over, it'd become a place of many firsts. Firsts that could happen here again—a new society could thrive, one that I'd always envisioned. A society my friend Sloan and I naively believed possible before. What a significant portion of our college years had been spent fighting for.

Monterey had set the stage for entertainment, creating the first theater in California; they'd publicly funded their schools and libraries. California's first printing press. I let myself see what Prescott and Jax saw, let my veil of pessimism drop for a moment. Jax's gaze lingered on my face for a moment longer than necessary. My cheeks flushed red-hot under his scrutiny.

"As much as I'd love to understand what the hell your two eyes are glazing over about, I've accepted that I just wasn't meant to."

My mouth opened. Though I was quick, ready to offer a snarky response, he beat me to it. "And before you say 'Jaxyboy, if you don't take the time to remember history, you'll simply make the same mistakes of the past,' I get it. Doesn't matter. If you're in, then I'm in. I don't have to understand, or even know, what you and Prescott have already conjured up inside your overly imaginative minds, but I'm so in. Whatever the future is here, it's surely better than the world we live in now."

His eyes met mine as he moved to squeeze my hand, dropping it at the awkwardness before moving on to Prescott, playfully shoving his shoulder. "Would be nice to see the good guys in charge for once."

Good. He thinks I'm good.

We'd had two tents to travel with, one with the capacity for a singular person, and one that held two. Prescott snored, which meant there'd been many, many nights for Jax and I to drown out our misery and air our dirty laundry. I'd bared my soul to him and he still believed there was good left inside. Admired me even, put me on a pedestal. Always pushing me to see what I was capable of. That the past was the past, I didn't have to let it define me or shape me. That I could create something beautiful from the trauma and that some of the most beautiful art in the world was built with broken pieces.

I scrunched my nose, letting my skepticism twist their nerves as I signaled to the view at our backs. "Cliffside over there *would* play to our benefit defensively during whatever inevitable war or political pissing match happens. Especially once the greedy assholes jump on your land grabbing bandwagon in a few months. Beach too. Something tells me that'll come in handy one day."

"Here I was thinking you'd mention having a nice view." Prescott faced me, an exasperated look on his face.

A hearty laugh pressed past Jax's rose-tinted lips. "And you call her 'sweet girl' because?"

"Because he squirms every time I call him Pops," I teased.

Prescott huffed sarcastically in response. "I could never take ownership of the work your father did on a headache like yourself."

Silence fell as the weight of my decision hung heavy in the air.

"Only right we follow tradition, I guess," I said, searching for the right words. "So, Monterey next then?"

Jax and Prescott grinned at each other. Jax handed him the extra bag of coffee he'd found from his pack. A bet clearly having been made behind my back. Harley came bounding over, dying down from a spell of zoomies, her muted barks demanding, causing Jax to reach back in and toss her a piece of dried meat.

I rolled my eyes. "Et tu, Harley?" A giggle escaped my lungs as I bent down to rub between her ears. I was outnumbered, but for once, in a way that made me feel safe.

The company around me was hopeful. Promising. I pushed back the feeling of unworthiness that crept up every time I experienced a tinge of happiness. *You deserve this. There is no shame in being a survivor, in living despite the odds.* The pain I harbored didn't have to consume me.

If history showed anything at all, when one empire

falls, another stronger one would rise in its place. But only if the conditions were right. If the people that picked up the pieces used the knowledge of the past, the good, the bad, the ugly, and the downfall and chose to learn from it. Chose to create a more perfect version. I could do the same, could give the same to others. Could atone for the sins of my past and never let another life end before it had the chance to truly begin.

I flipped them off, pretending to be annoyed with the way they always managed to team up. They were fit to create a place for the hopeful, for those seeking a new place to call home. Butterflies filled my stomach at the thought, happiness filling the once bottomless pit of despair. Shaking my head, I picked my bag off the ground and walked toward the center of a city made of ash.

And we began to build anew.

Part Three

THE SHADOW

Lessons Hard Lived

RILEY

I couldn't save her.

That was my biggest fear. One I'd prayed never came to fruition. Yet, as I watched her in her fitful sleep, I knew that I could not hold on forever.

She was sick. We had no food, no weapons. Only weapons of our minds. The freakish shit reality had erupted around us that day as I'd made my way back to the market bench. I'd been prepared to explain to my sister why the courts had shot down custody for the third and final time.

London had no home to go to. No place for us to gather what we would need to run for what seemed like the rest of our lives. I had failed her in more ways than one. My own home life had been unstable. After being kicked out of the group home when I aged out of the system, I'd spent every dime I'd earned on legal fees trying to get my sister out. It'd screwed me over in the end. What I was able to afford with the spare change of my checks wasn't survivable according to California law.

None of that mattered anymore. Except it did. I still couldn't provide for her, protect her. She was weak now. Dying. We were starving and had been for a while now. Supply out on the road had run dry. Over a year into the end of the world and anything easily accessible had been thoroughly raided in the area. So I'd said screw it. The Bay hadn't had much left for us, anyway. Not for a long time. Heading south seemed to be a good idea in the moment, but I'd severely underestimated the vast geography California possessed. We weren't equipped to make the journey—it was a lesson I was finding hard lived.

Figuring out how to control my magic should have remained my focus. Earth had powered me, but the ability to make it bend to my will remained impossible. I'd not had success in using it for any meaningful purpose. Only if we came across an edible plant could I make it grow. Once I depleted the source of its nutrients, that was it. Forget duplicating it or growing it from the conjures of my imagination.

It'd been my idea to stay near the road for the night. The woods on the other side of us were far too dense to find our way back out with the amount of energy we had left. Tomorrow, I would leave her tucked away and scour a few miles for something edible. Anything that could fill our stomachs. At least this place had makeshift weapons, though it bore no food. The fireplace poker would do well enough, and I could break the legs from the chair and carve out some spears once we came across another knife.

London had beat herself up for leaving behind the pack that contained our weapons, but she was hardly to blame. It was on me just as well for not noticing. My primary focus had been getting us off the road with the herd. Going back for it wasn't worth the risk.

I placed my palm on the hardwood floor. The fire ants surrounding a sticky splotch raced toward my fingertips. The tickle of them against my skin was soothing. This gift of mine confused me. Prior to the fall of civilization, I'd never minded bugs per se. There tended to be a lot of them in the homes we'd stayed in throughout our life, but the comfort they brought me now made no sense. In some moments, it felt as though they whispered to me.

Impossible.

Except it wasn't. In fact, it was expected. That's how my luck went.

Not much was known about our father outside of vague memories and what the files our social worker kept was able to relay to us overtime. One thing was consistent. Voices. He always heard voices. Eventually, the voices became too much. 911 was the first number my mother had taught me at the ripe age of eight. I'd put it to use that same year. Still, I was too late. I could not protect her. I could not protect him. I protected my sister, but everyone else, I'd failed.

Never again.

The world was so quiet now that the dead and the walking ruled it. It'd made the skill I'd learned early on in life easier to tune. The gravel at the edge of the driveway clanked under the pressure of heavy footsteps. Several footsteps. Fast ones. A man was through the door before I made it to my feet. He was fast, strong, one of the freakishly large ones. Like a feral cat, he pounced and sent us tumbling to the floor. Defending myself was instinctual, but in this weakened state I found myself useless. Slow. I was too damn slow for it to be an even match.

As the first blow connected with my temple, a sharp explosion of pain seared through my skull. The world spun in my momentarily disoriented state. Warm blood trickled down the side of my face, the cool ground beneath me screwing with my senses. Overstimulated was an understatement. Loud, nonrhythmic banging reverberated through the room. Every sound—every sense—was magnified. The frantic tempo of desperation and impending danger sped up the pounding of my heart. I needed to slow things down, regain control.

My hands dragged against the rough texture of the floor, betraying me as I struggled to regain my footing. The room seemed to tilt. A dizzying sensation sent me to my ass once more. Hands wrapped around my ankle and dragged me across the floor toward the door. The scent of decay hung heavy in the air, a sickly sweet reminder of what lay on the other side of the door. A hiss sang through the man's teeth. My fire ants sought to defend me as they crawled up his arm and clamped down on his skin.

Despite the chaos raging around me, I remained focused on London. Her eyes were wide with terror as she watched the struggle unfold. A surge of determination swept through me. I would not die here today. Not without making sure my sister was safe first.

Fighting against the pain and confusion, I flipped myself over and freed myself from his grasp. He fell on top of me, granting me the first clear look at him. His brown eyes were dark as coal. As cold as coal too. The hardness there was familiar to me. I knew that look. A survivor's stare.

"Wait," I mumbled, using most of my remaining strength to shove him off me.

The man stumbled back, his hand instinctively reaching for the gun holstered at his side. My heart sank to my ass. I lunged forward, grappling with him in a frantic struggle for control.

"Kill him, Riley," my sister croaked as she pushed herself against the fireplace behind her. She rolled to her knees, attempting to get up and failing.

His fingers closed around the grip of his pistol. The cold metal bit into my skin as I fought him off. Adrenaline powered me, dulling the agony of my injuries. But the man was strong. His grip unyielding.

"Here." A fireplace poker clanged against the ground. "Finish him."

No. It couldn't be that simple. If all we did was kill

each other, then the dead would win. We needed to work together, play to each other's strengths. A group with a survivor's mentality would be a force to be reckoned with. It wasn't that long ago when my sister recognized that as the truth.

With a desperate cry, I threw myself forward and drove my shoulder into his chest. My fingers laced around the poker. I slammed it into his hand, sending the gun flying across the room. The impact staggered him.

"We don't have to fight. We can help each other," I tried again between ragged breaths.

London coughed, leaning forward as she dug through her bag, likely for her knife. "It's us or them, Ril."

"*This* is how we survive, London. This is how I make sure you live. We need help. We can help each other."

"Help?" the man choked out a laugh. "In this world?"

I seized the opportunity. Tackling him to the ground, I placed him in a choke hold. I wasn't sure where the strength found me, but I was glad it did.

For a heartbeat, we stayed locked in the deadly embrace. Breathless and bruised, I loosened my hold as his struggle stopped. "Yeah, in this world. We're safer as three than we are as two or alone."

He tapped my arm in yield and I released him. "Have you seen the groups out here? Nothing but trouble. More people, more noise, more zombies."

"I said three, not twenty."

"I just attacked you to leave you as live bait to those zombie shits clawing through the door," he muttered. The beanie he'd worn fell off in our tumble, revealing his stark white hair.

"Unfortunately, I can't say being left out as bait hasn't been a common theme in my life."

Consideration teased at his pale features. Everything about the guy seemed cold, but I didn't care. "You have no clue the kind of person I am," he said.

"We'd be a team. The only thing I need to know is that we have the same goal; staying alive. We"—I nodded toward London, who only glared back at me—"are no strangers to survivor pacts. Been at it for a long time."

This had been a point of contention for us since the beginning. It'd pretty much been the two of us outside of one instance. It had only been a few weeks and despite the outcome, it'd been worth it. London had become attached to April. I might have even said she'd come to see her as more than a friend or ally, though she'd claimed there was no time for that.

Part of the time, London appeared more equipped for this life than I was. I was supposed to be the one protecting her yet more times than not, she'd been the one to make all the decisions. I just wanted to keep her happy. I couldn't do that before, but I could do it now even with the world going to shit. Until recently. When her health had declined. Now all I cared about was keeping her safe. *Alive*. April's presence had increased our security, allowing us to cover more ground in search of food and weapons.

"You know my vote is to kill you," London grumbled,

and I realized his attention had fallen to her. "Lucky I can't do it myself."

There was no time for contemplation. The door burst open, thudding against the wall like thunder clapping through a silent night. The dead flood into the room, the sickening clicks and groans echoing. A macabre symphony of death. Panic took over. My once logical line of thinking abandoned me for the first time since I was eight. London whimpered, desperate to push herself away from the advancing herd. Her efforts were futile.

I scanned the room for the gun. They were fast. Too fast to have given us a fighting chance of all walking out alive. I swung the poker, driving the bar through their decaying skulls. The man fought at my back, the slicing of metal on skin giving me the impression he also carried a knife. London's shrill cry for help overtook the moans of death that danced through the air.

Through the bodies of the dead, I'd lost sight of her.

The bar caught on bone, stuck within the skull of the lost soul in front of me. I let go. Dropping to the ground, I searched for something else to use. Anything.

The man dropped with me. "Do you have a plan?" he asked.

He passed me a knife as we kicked back the dead that had fallen atop of us in their reach for our bodies to feast on. A glimmer of metal caught my eye near the couch.

"No plan except to survive." Without hesitation, I scrambled for it, grabbing hold as the man fought off the advancing dead.

I held steady as I aimed and fired. The splintering sound of gunfire sang around the room as I fought to clear a path to the cries of my sister. London's screams grew faint and hope soared through me. She only had to kill the first few and drop the body of the dead atop her to cover her scent.

The magazine emptied, and I cursed under my breath.

"Catch," the man offered, throwing an extra mag toward me.

My reflexes failed me as it tumbled to the floor. I reached down, emptying the first one, then shoved the re-up in. Four shots rang out and then the room went silent. With a sickening finality, the dead that had surrounded her tumbled to the ground. Blood spurted. Crimson painting the room as the life of my sister faded away before my eyes. The bite mark on her leg went down to the bone, and blood pooled out in an impossibly large puddle.

London's jaw was slack, a terrifying rattle releasing from her chest as the bursts of blood slowed to a dribble from the side of her neck. The last pumps of her heart were not strong enough to continue painting the walls the color my little sister bled.

In a cry of anguish, I fell to my knees, crawling to her as I fired round after round into the skulls of the dead, leaving all but one in the chamber. It didn't matter. No amount of gunfire could bring her back. I took a deep, controlled breath. I was truly alone in this unforgiving world. As I stood amid the carnage of London's corpse, it dawned on me that nothing would ever be the same again.

Eyes brimmed with tears, I turned to look at the man I'd extended a hand to moments before. *This is not his fault,* I attempted to reason with myself. It was mine. It was my sister. I was the one to protect her.

Except without him, none of this would have ever happened.

He raised his hands. His words of apology fell on deaf ears as I met his steely gaze. The apology was to keep his life, it would not bring her back. Nothing would. The only way my sister could live on is through me. Through living in her honor.

Without a word, I raised the gun, the weight of it now heavy in my trembling hand. There was no mercy to be found in this broken, screwed up world. I silenced his apologies forever. Nothing. I felt nothing as I watched his body crumple to the ground.

Another deep breath in. And out. I closed my eyes, willing myself to focus. I couldn't change the past, but I could keep moving forward. For London. I would keep living for London. She would want that. My sister, who was so full of life, determined to survive no matter the cost. She was right; there was something to be said about sticking to the shadows, to being on our own.

I walked over to London's lifeless body. Kneeling beside her, I gently brushed a dark brown curl from her face, the touch of it breaking off a piece of my heart. I pulled the blanket she'd been sleeping with over her body and tucked it in at her sides. An eternal slumber. The last time I'd ever tuck her in.

Whispering a solemn goodbye, I turned away from the only family I'd ever known and left my world behind. London had been my everything for the last sixteen years. I'd sworn to keep her safe.

I had failed.

The Quiet Ones

RILEY

The last sunrays of the day filtered into the cave, the glow elongating the shadows of the critters that accompanied me everywhere. I crouched over a small fire I managed to kindle from dry branches. This was the part I hated the most. When there were no fish and the ants found their way back to me empty-handed.

There was a short time where surviving had become easier. Fish had begun to repopulate the Pacific and streams. Depending on the luck of the day, I could catch enough to hold myself over for a day or two. In the moments when I'd come home empty, my ants brought me what they could. Small crumbs, occasional edible plants. Those were always trial and error.

My magic, while useful in life or death situations, had

failed me when it came to food. The plants I grew were poisonous each and every time. I wasn't sure if it was due to a lack of control, my less than ideal health, or just how the earth had punished me for surviving. Bringing myself near death twice had deterred any further efforts in determining the *why*.

When times were desperate, when food had evaded me for days, they offered up themselves. Ants, crickets, grasshoppers, inch worms if it rained the night before. Protein was key. Though I wasn't quite sure what the point of surviving was. If there was really nothing left in this fallen world, then what was I fighting for? It wasn't giving up. Acceptance is perseverance in disguise.

A rock tumbled into the fire from behind me, my body tensing, trying to get a sense of the threat behind me. Whoever it was had been silent in their approach. A threat. Only predators sneak up on their prey. I turned, hand going to the ax strapped across my back. Her appearance caught me off guard. The innocence in her face didn't match the lethal confidence of her demeanor.

"Pansies don't scare me, but those little shits you have crawling up your arm are enough to send me in the other direction." Her raspy voice bounced off the cold, stone walls of the cave as she stepped into the entrance. "Is it hard? Eating your friends?"

Drawing my weapon, I flipped it in my palm and shifted positions. With the sun streaming in at an angle, it put me at a disadvantage I wasn't keen on keeping.

"Relax. If I wanted to hurt you, I would've done that

hours ago," the woman remarked casually. The slight in her voice carried a hint of amusement.

Her boldness set me off kilter, unsure of how to respond. She stepped further into the cave, arms crossed over her tank top that was tucked into some black cargo pants. A small armory lined the belt of her pants, but her energy made me feel as though there was more to fear from her than the weapons at her side.

I scanned the rest of her as she set down a backpack at her feet. "You should really be more aware of your surroundings." Her dark hair was pulled into a tight bun, everything about her was a bit *too* put together to be out here on her own.

"You're clean," I observed, taking note of the lack of overall grime over her body. Even underneath her finger-nails was absent the usual caked clump of both earth and flesh.

"So observant."

Smoke and ash filled the air around me, yet the truth was evident. "No smell." My eyes narrowed. "You don't stink."

"How kind," she surmised, hand falling to her chest in feigned flattery.

"What do you want?"

There was no denying the woman before me was a force of nature. While she appeared a few years younger than me, a pinch in my gut set off the warning bells in my mind. The way she stood there—a mixture of defiance and vulnerability in her stance—I found myself intrigued. Still, I wouldn't ignore my gut. Not again.

The tension between us hung sharply in the air. I edged to the side, sizing her up. Shifting my weight, I glanced around the cavern walls. In this confined space, every move mattered and an advantage could be the difference between life or death. Her gaze was unwavering as she met my eyes. Everything about her seemed calculated.

"For you to come back with me to Monterey." The woman's round lips curled into a smirk, a hint of the wild in her wide eyes.

Frustration flickered through me. The emotion was so fleeting, it caught me off guard. There was something innately trustworthy about the woman standing before me, yet her choice to lie made it wane. "Monterey burned to the ground."

"Odd thing to tell someone who literally passed through its very gates this morning. You know something I don't?"

I struggled to maintain a facade of disinterest, but could sense my uncertainty lingering beneath the surface. We stood there, locked in wordless curiosity. She closed some of the gap between us with a few purposeful steps. Her head tilted, a curl popping free in her bun. I looked down at her, though the command in her presence made it feel as if we met eye to eye.

"How long have you been on your own?"

"I'm not alone," I lied.

She scanned the cave in a dramatic display before

smirking. "Oh, come on, don't lie to me. Not a great way to establish trust."

"Ninety-two days."

While my focus remained locked on the micro-change in her body language, the quickness of my response shocked even myself. Maybe it was loneliness. Maybe it was because I was so damn tired. But I wanted to tell her my story against my better judgment.

Don't. Remember what happened. You'll fail her too.

"That's very precise. You count the days like that often?"

The fire crackled in the empty air. Embers floated around the cave as the flames dimmed. She took a deep breath, tapping her fingers against her pants in contemplation. Looking toward the gray smoke trickling out of the cave, the fire erupted back to its original state. A firecaster then.

"Well, that explains a lot," she continued when I offered no response. "You're misinformed. Sad reality of leaving behind a group."

"I don't leave people behind," I hissed, angered by the insinuation.

I would never leave someone behind. That wasn't an option for me. Once a team, always a team. No matter what, no matter the costs.

I would not fail.

She took two steps forward, closing what remained of the gap while carefully avoiding the critters on the group. Placing a hand on my shoulder, she swallowed a gag as the ants at my feet crawled up my leg toward my arm. "Didn't peg you for the kind of guy that did. Just making sure."

Backing away, she kept her steps even paced. Her foot backed into the bag she'd dropped at the entrance. Slowly, she pulled it up and opened it. Wide brown eyes held steady on mine as she pulled out a canteen and a pack of nuts. A piece of jerky wrapped in cloth landed on top, causing my mouth to water. It'd been a long time since I'd had any meat that didn't come from the sea.

"Sorry, it sucks. We're just now getting into the whole quality food stuff." Her eyes flickered as she gauged my reaction. "Name's Amaia. I'm from a group over in Monterey. We're putting up walls, rebuilding. Ya know, trying out the whole civilization idea again if you're into that kind of thing."

"You're inviting a stranger to come stay in your home?"

It didn't make any sense. So far, all the groups I'd come across had been nothing but trouble. My sister was right, staying to ourselves had been the best course of action. If only I had followed the path. There weren't many good people left in this world. Weren't many good people to begin with.

"Well, it's a community, not a house, and you're not a stranger if I've spent the last day watching you. I know enough." Mischief sang in her tone as she spoke of her antics, leaning her body against the wall of the cave. "Followed you back from the Pacific. It's not that you're bad at covering your trail. Actually got me lost a few times before

I picked it up again. You just aren't good enough to keep away someone looking for a guy like *you*."

Who was protecting this woman? Who had her back? The work she was doing was dangerous. Not because she was a woman, but because she was alone. Amaia's mindset was risky. Taking in strangers, accepting the unknown would end up with her hurt or worse. Flashes of London's last moments sauntered around my mind, teasing me with pangs of guilt. If no one had Amaia's back, then I would. Someone had to look out for her.

I glanced her over once more. Really *studied* her this time. Inspected every inch of her being as she watched, letting me see what I needed to. She kept one arm down at her side, the other on her hip, leaving herself vulnerable to my scrutiny. A small smile graced her lips. This time, however, the smile was kind, pure. Honest. Screamed an honest woman. Pure hearts never got you far these days, but what did I have to lose from finding out what she had to offer?

"How many of you?"

"No more than a thousand," she answered, shrugging as she considered a passing thought. "Though that'll probably change when Jax gets back tonight. He was tracking a decent group a few miles east for a while."

Peering behind her, I wondered if she did in fact have someone accompanying her. If she did, they'd kept themselves well-hidden during our interaction. No one was there. Moments passed, and I listened for any hints. The only response was the crashing of waves and nature in the distance. Not sure who the hell Jax was, I loosened my posture, deciding to see where this next phase in life had to offer me.

"You can bring your stuff with you." Amaia chuckled, taking a few steps back and leaving the backpack at the cave entrance. "There's more food in there. Try not to eat it too fast or you'll make yourself sick. I'll be back in a day. I need to make some arrangements."

"I didn't say yes," I called after her, watching her disappear around the corner and out of sight.

"Yes, you did," Amaia's voice chimed over the angry waves below the cliff side. "Maybe not right now, but your mind will change by the time I get back."

I considered following her for a moment. A brief moment, but nevertheless, considered. Spooking her was the last thing I wanted. Amaia hadn't been kind necessarily, but she was forward in her intentions. I respected that. Respected her for offering me the opportunity. She was right, I hadn't decided to go with her yet. Physically. But mentally, I was there. Ready to accept whatever the future looked like.

Women had enough to worry about in this world—a man following her along the coastline didn't to be another. I wasn't sure how she would respond to that or the kind of magic she had, but I knew what I had and I didn't want to hurt her. The joyous youth that remained in her eyes stroked that hopeful string in my heart that had lain dormant for God knows how long.

No. That wasn't true. I did know. Since London died.

Maybe it was her spirit speaking to me, driving me to follow my heart again when I'd long abandoned it for my head. I could trust Amaia. And now I would need her to trust me. If Monterey was truly a place meant for me, she would come back. No matter how agonizing the next twenty-four hours would become.

On the ninety-third day alone, I found my forever home.

She came back the next morning. The sun's position blinded me as my eyes cracked open. Her shadow crawled across the cavern wall. A tall man stalked behind her, his eyes shifting about. It took him a few moments before they passed over me. I shot up under his intense stare. Sharp, hazel eyes hovered on mine. We remained locked in a stand-off, the threat passing between us clear: *Hurt her and die*. I nodded in reassurance. There would be no threat from me.

He cleared his throat for a false pleasantry. "How are you getting on?"

"See, I told you it'd make a good hideout," Amaia said, splitting the tension.

"I'm not sure a cave where you can spy *in* without them knowing is a good hideout." His vowels stretched while he tripped over other portions of words, making it hard to place his accent. If I had to guess, he'd been in the country for a while before the bombs went off.

"Oh please, I never would've found this place had I

not followed him from the wharf." She paused thought-fully, stopping in front of me with a container in her hand. "Also, fire is always a bad idea unless 'you're desperate."

The familiarity with which she communicated with me was not overlooked. When she spoke to me, it was as if we were long-lost friends. Now in the group of three, she moved between the red-haired man and me with relaxed shoulders. His attention on me was unwavering though it was clear he tracked each of her movements.

"She's a wee hardheaded. Apologies for the intrusion lad, ready to go?" His use of slang clued me in, though now that I looked him over, it was obvious.

My silence persisted despite my best wishes. It was overwhelming being around others after spending so much time alone. While I hadn't been out there solo as long as others and it was only two of them, it still felt like a crowd. *No, you made your decision. Stick to it.*

Amaia cleared her throat, offering a small smile. Today she'd come more casual. Her hair was down, the dark curls falling in front of her face, and she sported shorts instead of cargo pants to accommodate the heat of the day. She hadn't lost the small armory around her body, however.

"This is Jax. My friend I told you about yesterday. We trust him, okay?" With a gentle push, Amaia placed the container against my chest. Her gaze shot toward the ground as she peered in Jax's direction. By the way his freckled face reddened at his name on her lips, 'friend' didn't seem to be the right word. "For your little friends. Thought you should probably stop eating them."

For the first time in ninety-eight days, I laughed. A small, inaudible laugh, but a laugh nonetheless. It had been ninety-three days since London died. Ninety-five since I'd accepted she might not get better. And ninety-eight since she fell sick.

You can't put yourself through this again. This is wrong. Leave in the night. Stick to the shadows.

I shook my head, wrestling with the thoughts and doing my best to discern logic from fallacy. The facts. All I needed to do was focus on the facts at hand. The rest I could deal with once I had all the information I needed to make an informed decision. That would mean seeing the place firsthand, really looking into what they had to offer. Amaia and Jax seemed healthy enough. Clean. Well put together. More importantly, there was a peace in her eyes that I hadn't seen in over a year and a half. Since the world ended.

"If your home is safe, why do you need a hideout?" I questioned, circling back to her first observation when she arrived.

Jax cracked a crooked smile. "Because she's got a few screws loose."

A sharp, childlike chuckle escaped Amaia as she stepped toward Jax and shoved him playfully. "*No.* Because one can never be too prepared," she said, her tone shifting back to one of authority. "Sometimes you end up shit out of luck. A stocked up hideaway can prevent that."

"You must have resources to spare if you can stand the risk of someone else taking it."

Amaia shrugged while Jax released an amused snort like it was not a big deal that it was. Resources were slim. Every calorie counted. Leaving something for the next person may end up causing your own death.

"That's kinda the point," Amaia offered. "At the end of the day it's how humanity will survive. Whether it's for our people or someone else, at least it'll go toward someone in need."

Opening the container, I commanded the ants to make their way inside. A few curious stray critters joined them and I wondered if my command had reached them too. I still wasn't clear on how many I could have under my control at once, but maybe the safety of a home would allow me the space to explore the full extent of my gifts. Amaia had jabbed small air holes over the top. Although she didn't appear to have the same appreciation toward my small friends, the gesture meant everything.

I reached for my belongings, but Jax beat me there. "We have to start caring less about ourselves and more for the good of the group. Do you ever wonder how far the human race could have gone had we kept that idea as a guiding force?" Tossing one of my bags over his shoulder, another sly grin tugged at his lips followed by a pat on the back as he strolled out the cave. It was harder to read him than it was her. Still there was a welcoming aura in the protectiveness he offered her.

My heart palpitated. The sore, aching place in my heart saddened my sister would not be here for this. What-ever *this* was.

Amaia walked at my side, keeping my hesitant pace. A constant, small smile populated her face. I watched as she followed behind Jax who's head remained on a constant swivel. The sun shined against her sepia skin. *Grateful.* That was the emotion she wore that radiated from her. Not peace, but grateful for another chance. It was comforting.

We walked in only the white noise of nature for miles, the landscape stretching on in desolate ruins. Somewhere between being lost in my thoughts and Jax's whistles a dog had appeared at Amaia's side. She was large with a healthy shine to her coat. The animal sniffed at my ankles as I walked before taking off on ahead of our group. It wasn't until a gust of wind brushed against my skin that the faint whispers of my surroundings sunk in. The horizon ahead was broken by the sight of looming steel walls and the distant dance of smokestacks.

Despite the obvious signs of construction, an eerie quiet hung in the air. The realization dawned on me. This community had harnessed their powers to rebuild, the wind dispersing the noise of construction in order to spread out any incoming herds.

I spiraled. My thoughts varying from utter amazement to a horrid question of whose bed I was offering to lay in.

Amaia bumped her shoulder into mine with an understanding stare. "You don't talk?"

"I prefer to listen," I mumbled, and it was true. There was no need to speak when people's intentions often became clear if you just sat back to listen. To watch, much to Amaia's point.

"They say it's the quiet ones you have to watch," Jax said, slowing to match his pace to ours.

Glancing at Amaia, I took my chance to make a boundary clear. "I also prefer to do the watching."

"We'll work on that then," she teased. "Because you're not very good at it."

"Or maybe I am."

"Was that a joke?" Amaia grinned, the Doberman ahead of her barking as we approached a gap in the wall.

I didn't answer her. Didn't need to. Instead, I stepped through what felt to be a portal to a new home. As long as it was her home, it would be mine. For I would protect this place with everything I had, protect Amaia. Construction had consumed this area of stone homes and cobbled roads but within a few steps I knew it was everything London and I had searched for our entire lives. It was a haven. In this life, it was hard to tell who was who in the world before. But here, it didn't appear to matter as a village of people worked to put this place together. They greeted Amaia and Jax as I walked through. Each of them nodded toward me in silent hello then turned back to their duties paying me no mind. Laughs erupted between the young and old, but more importantly, there was no sign of distress.

This place was a haven. A place to call home. Amaia's vision was mine, and thus, she was mine to protect.

And I would not fail.

A Dark Place

RILEY

"You were never crazy, Ril."

Heavy breaths passed between us as Amaia ran at my side. I picked up my pace, training before lunch had become a routine. It was my favorite time of the day since it was just the two of us. The temperature along the coast of Monterey had finally tempered though we couldn't be sure if it was the season or Earth starting to heal. With as many scientists and researchers that had arrived lately —*Scholars* or whatever people had been calling them— maybe the answers would come soon.

"You don't know that," I said after another quarter mile.

She'd been pushing the issue of the bugs and my mental health the last few weeks. With The Compound being so quiet lately, Amaia had grown bored. Her boredom happened to lead to an interest in my personal affairs. It wasn't like she didn't have things to do to pass time but deflection of her own problems was her MO. Problems like her relationship with Jax.

"Except I do," she chided, picking up the pace as we crossed through an old golf course. "And now, you know it too."

Only the kick up from the recently laid cobblestone of this corner in The Compound responded to her statement. What was there for me to say? She was right. Science had never been one of my strong suits, but I wasn't an idiot. There were indisputable facts, hard science, and then there was what your mind wanted you to believe as fact. I was struggling with the latter. We waved at one of the newer couples from the San Antonio area as they stepped out the most recent duplex builds.

Monterey Revival Style, Jax had labeled it. The Culture and Customs Committee he was intent on forming had decided to designate a living area filled with inspiration from residents' hometowns. Of course I'd heard Amaia whisper the concept in his ear over dinner, but her thoughts often rolled into his.

"Why is this the one thing you refuse to accept?" she accused after another lap of silence.

My lips pursed to the side. Though there was a very straightforward answer to that question, if I voiced it aloud, I would have to address it. At times I felt ready for that, times such as now when Amaia was by my side. It was the reason she'd sought out one of the doctors for an opinion at my request. Then there were the moments I was alone with my thoughts. When the realization that the wrong answer to the questions I sought after could end up haunting me forever.

"Because."

A strong gust of wind slapped me across the face. La Niña had kicked up in aggression with the instability of the atmosphere.

"Because." Amaia broke into a full sprint. "Why?"

"Because if I accept it, then I'll let my guard down."

"Letting your guard down never killed anyone," she came to a complete halt as the words passed through her ill-filtered lips. "Poor joke."

I shrugged, coming to a stop a few steps ahead. The same could be said for her. "Only if you're laughing at yourself too."

"Ha, funny," Amaia grumbled and turned down a path leading to another portion of the now fully enclosed Compound.

They'd closed off most of what would have been considered Monterey city-proper in what Amaia referred to as The Before. It was her way of separating realities. We were not the people life had molded us to be before society collapsed. Those who remained the same, died. It was simple. The same could be said for the city of Monterey, the people here were determined to rise from the ashes. We would never be who we were Before but it was who we were in The After that would make all the difference.

A large glass building sat in the center of The

Compound next to The Gardens. It wasn't complete with all the rooms Jax had instructed them to add on. So we ate most meals under an awning that an Earth elemental constructed to keep us shielded. *The Kitchens*, the Customs and Culture committee had settled on, was far too big for our current population. I still found it an illogical allocation of resources but I wasn't in charge. I understood the line of thinking though. With the violence of the world slowing down and trade networks securely established, population growth was inevitable—especially if this test of society proved to be sustainable.

"I'm being serious though, Riley," Amaia pressed on. Her persistence was oddly endearing. "It's time to accept the truth for what it is, a gift."

Rolling my eyes, the words slipped past my lips without a second thought. "This has never been a gift." The response was reflexive.

"Then make it one."

"How do you mean?" I asked, admittedly curious on her perspective.

"You know, bend that shit to your advantage. Use it to fuel you, to do whatever it is here that you want to do." I listened as she spoke, her tone shifted to one that was definitive. I wouldn't be able to fight her on this. Not anymore. "It's time. You've been here for half a year and while everyone's found their job, their home—"

"I haven't."

"You have," she said, side-eyeing me. Snapping at her never ended well. Much like London, it was better to bite my tongue and let her say her piece. "My home is your home, you know that. But now you need to find your place. Not just physically, I mean, here at The Compound. It's time to settle in."

"Been spending a lot of time with Prescott lately?" I muttered, it sounded more like his words than hers and she had a bad habit of regurgitating his opinion.

It wasn't something I blamed her for. She was young, not exactly impressionable but Prescott had a lot of knowledge to share. I only wished she put a little more faith in her own line of thinking. There was a lot of pressure though with her being a founding member of The Compound. People looked to her with a certain sense of authority. Saying the wrong thing could make all this shit collapse. The saying 'Rome didn't fall in a day' was stupid because it did. All it took was one bad decision, and the rest was a trickle-down effect.

"Well, yes," she said, her head tilting side to side as she thought through her next words. "But my point is still valid. You were never crazy, Riley. Your father was never crazy, according to Henry, the symptoms presented as schizophrenia."

"Can I tell you something I've never voiced out loud?"

"Always." Her voice was gentle, soft, as she took my hand and gave it a light squeeze.

"I knew that," I said, reflecting back on my childhood. "From the time I was a kid ... Just if I said it out loud, it made it real."

"Denial isn't really your thing."

Huffing a laugh, I looped my arm around her shoulder, pulling her in for what had become a comforting embrace over the last few months. "Don't I know it."

Henry was a surgeon in The Before but here at The Compound he was multi-faceted. If others with healing gifts or medical training in the past ended up settling here, he could go back to his specialty. With his wife as a former psychiatrist, Amaia had asked them to team up and run some tests, ultimately landing on the diagnosis. Well, a lack thereof. I was not schizophrenic, but my father was, so it would remain a possibility for the next few years until I aged out the range. The whispers I heard were true, and the shadows were my answer. The bugs spoke to me, awaited my command. No one else had these gifts that we were aware of.

"We can't tell anyone."

"I know." She nodded. "Henry and Margot won't say anything either. We'll protect you, don't worry."

I shook my head. That wasn't my concern. Yeah, there were people out there who still hunted down those who had more power than them. They ran in groups and often overtook smaller ones to 'secure their survival.' Survival of the fittest had taken a tragic turn. Some even claimed they'd seen them tossed into the back of caravans that were headed east. Rumors were of no importance to me, but facts, facts I could work with and I knew exactly how to get them.

We approached the construction site of what would be The Kitchens in a few months. Jax waved to us from the spot we'd become accustomed to eating most of our meals at, though at times the two of them disappeared into Prescott's quarters through dinner and late into the night. I gripped her wrist, halting her in our approach. She turned, staring up at me in question at the hold up.

"You're right. It's time I do more around here. Pull my weight in a more consistent way."

"Feels like there's a 'but' coming somewhere," she said as she nibbled on her bottom lip.

"That's a given," I chided, peering down at the person who saved me in more ways than one. A deeper dive into our vulnerable side wasn't something the two of us shared often. We'd been in sync since the day I'd arrived. But there were moments like this when it was important to get the words out. Important to make it clear where I stood, where my priorities lied. "My mind … it's a dark place, yet you brighten it."

"Oh shit, are we having a moment?" Amaia chuckled only to be silenced by the simmer of my glare. "Right, sorry. Go ahead."

"If this is truly a gift I possess, then I want to use it to help you. To keep this place safe."

She took a step closer to me, the scent of ash and coffee filling the space between us. A heavy look of concern hung in her dark eyes. "You mean keep *me* safe? We talked about this. Compound first. I'm a big girl, Ril, I can handle myself."

"Don't we all know it." I brushed off her response, tipping my head at the passersby headed to mealtime. In a hushed tone, I met her stare. "That doesn't mean you don't need someone to have your back."

"Well, there's two someones technically." She shrugged with a sigh. "Three if you include yourself. Not that any of you ever asked my permission to do that."

"And I still won't, but I'd like your blessing. Yes, there are two men at your back, but this place is going to be something someday. A symbol of what's possible. A good soldier has a plan A, B, and C. A soldier that *survives*—"

"Doesn't have plans, they possess an artillery of blueprints, knowledge and a solid team at their back." The smirk she so proudly wore crept onto her face she finished my sentence. It was the exact phrase she'd uttered this morning to the current, pompous general who was bound to get someone killed. "You've been working the shadows despite your concerns."

I held my head high, accepting the praise she always managed to provide no matter how small the accomplishment. Jax rose to his feet in the distance at the shift in my posture. His freckled face was reddened, a wide smile plastered across it. He was far more observant than the residents gave him credit for.

"You've shown no interest in being one of our soldiers."

"I'm not their soldier." I stood at attention, eyes trained on the daring woman before me. "I'm *your* weapon."

"Are you sure about this?" she whispered, but the

toothy grin shining back at me dimmed out any ounce of hesitancy that may have remained.

With a sharp chuckle, I saluted her. "What's my first mission, Lieutenant?"

"I thought you'd never ask."

Stick To The Shadows

RILEY

Remember who you are. If you do that, you have nothing to worry about. Those were the words Amaia had scribbled on a note stuck on the door of our shared space upon departure last night. She was on her way to a neighboring settlement in San Jose. This would be the first time she left Monterey since I'd arrived. Today was a new beginning. While my duties to Amaia had varied in nature, manning the gates had been newly appointed under my wing.

Prescott's suggestion to which I had politely declined until Amaia agreed that there was no better place to have her back than controlling who had access inside. Who we allowed a chance inside was up to me and my men. Our team was small—only Mohammed, me, and a handful of others—but it would fulfill our needs for now.

We couldn't go on this way forever. The planning was something I was still working out, but once we vetted the rest of the soldiers Amaia recommended, we'd be off to a solid start. A few weeks max.

The reminder to remember who I was hadn't come as a surprise. The past few months had left me questioning myself. Now that I had settled into my role and with Amaia and Jax spending an obsessive amount of time together, my spare moments were left for nothing but reflection. *Who was I really? Without my sister, without Amaia, without this place ... who was I? What did I want my future to look like?* Because I had that now, a future.

Mohammed shoved Jax into me as we made our way through The Compound after a sunrise training session. They laughed, Jax baiting Mohammed on the way his eye twitched as a tell before he tossed a kick in The Ring.

"Best you pray that when war comes knockin' at our doorstep, they aren't interested in a good brawl," Jax teased, only to be tripped up by Mohammed in jest.

"At least my girl can't put me on my ass."

I stifled a laugh at Mohammed's dig. For as long as I'd been here, I'd never seen Jax beat her in The Ring and it wasn't for his lack of trying. It was reassuring to say the least. With the constant clashing of different settlements over land or trade, *something* was brewing, though I wasn't sure war was quite it. It was why she'd left The Compound after all.

"I'm getting a bit worried, ya know?" Wrinkles formed around his eyes as he looked toward me. "You're there, we all share quarters. It's no secret Amaia's not sleeping again, and she's knocking back more than her fair share. She's spiraling. I know you, Riley. You've been hovering like a hawk, I know you see it."

"Seems to be the same Lieutenant from when I arrived if you ask me. If you want to be concerned, I'd worry about Banks making his move. He's been asking around about her. Wondering if it's official. Considering he went out on that mission with her ..." Mohammed said in an attempt to quiet the concerns and change course.

Jax freed himself from Mohammed's jerking grasp. "I'm working on it."

"Well, work harder," Mohammed said smugly, swiping his silky black hair back into a neater bun. "We've been settled a year, man. Almost ten thousand strong inside the walls, not counting the people nearby. Our defenses are good. Forget about stressing over the home front. I mean, come on, this is it. What are we waiting for? The world to fall apart all over again? Death? Screw that. I can't do 'what ifs' anymore. Thinking about starting a family, setting down some roots.

"Aye, really? Congrats." Jax's catlike eyes brightened in response.

"It's a simple thought for now," Mohammed said, though his disposition hadn't changed, the tone of his voice turned grave. "Yasmin and I are allowing Allah to bless us as intended."

Their chatter faded into the background. As much as I wanted Mohammed's hopefulness to provide me comfort,

I knew things were never that simple. To let your guard down was to give up. We needed to remain vigilant, *especially* because we had a lot to protect.

We rounded the corner, the recently completed Kitchens now in sight. The aroma of freshly baked bread and coffee wafted in the air and mixed with the medicinal flora near the entrance. It was such an adjustment compared to the last two years. Shit, an adjustment for damn near my entire life. This was the first time I'd had a stable, consistent source of food and housing in, well ... ever.

"I can count on you though." Jax nudged me gently. "Right, lad?"

Whatever the two of them were on about now didn't matter. Not when the hairs on the back of my neck raised in warning. I looked around. "Mhmm. Yeah, sure," I said as I scanned our immediate area.

A figure striding in a quick pace away from the other side of The Garden's nagged my attention. Fruit and a loaf of bread fell from his jacket. He was tall and lean, his skin the color of oak. Around sixteen if I had to guess. As if he sensed my eyes on him, he took off running, peering over his shoulder.

Neither Jax nor Mohammed showed any signs of noticing him. I sent a dragonfly after him, tracking where he was headed. Chasing after him felt wrong. I knew that look of starvation. The desperation that came with it. There was only one problem scratching that soft spot in my brain: if he's here, then he's safe. So why did he feel the need to steal?

Denial's not really your thing. Amaia was right, it wasn't. The situation was clear as day and I recognized it for what it was. That fear that if you didn't secure your next meal, then you risked the possibility of spending the rest of your life wondering if you would ever have one again. He was hoarding because he thought he had to. That lack of security in one's home and resources were damning. Infectious. And as sorry as I was for the kid, I couldn't let it spread.

Stick to the shadows, Riley, stick to the shadows.

Damnit. "I'll meet you there," I called over my shoulder as I swiveled on my heels. "Forgot Amaia asked me to bring Prescott some maps for daily stand up."

Taking off after him, I kept a slight jog until I was out of their view then upped my pace. Having undergone the slow and steady training process of mastering my gifts, I kept tabs on him through the whispers of the dragonfly passed on through space and time. Perhaps I would never truly understand how my gifts worked in totality. If that was how things were meant to be, then I wouldn't question it. There was a point in life when knowing *too* many answers to the questions of the universe became taxing. The line being drawn here was alright for now.

The newer construction of homes were brick cottage style homes made the feel of the area seem like a village straight out of a fairy tale. I'd been more of a space opera guy than fantasy, but from what Amaia described, it'd been executed perfectly. Medieval almost. This section hadn't been fully populated yet, the vacancy on many of the side streets apparent by the lack of various greenery outside the homes. Prescott had insisted on making the best use of all space even though we had The Gardens.

I didn't need the dragonfly to make me aware of where he ended up. The rebound of the door clued me in as I rounded the corner. Taking a deep breath, I did my best to keep my eyes open. Stumbling to a walk my focus held. It was imperative I learned to multitask as my mind was two places at once. Keeping my wits about me in my immediate surroundings was a life skill I couldn't abandon, yet knowing what awaited me inside before entering could be the difference between life or death.

There'd been virtually no crime here outside of emotion fueled fights regarding survival and close quarters. Things you'd expect when a large group of strangers that likely wouldn't have ever co-existed in the same space were now forced to learn to work together as a collective. To put their differences aside in favor of The Compound.

It took a moment for anything inside to answer my call but sure enough, an eight-legged friend did. I smiled in accomplishment. From the web in the corner of the front entrance, it relayed the message that he was alone. I crept toward the door and weighed over what to do next. On one hand, he was stealing from the group, which could not go uncorrected. On the other, Amaia had helped me as Prescott had helped her.

It doesn't matter. That's not your role. Your role is to

obey your orders and your orders are to protect this place. To protect her. You cannot protect her if you allow dissent. I shook off the thought, my locs slapping against my cheeks. He was a kid.

Stick to the shadows, London's words hammered. The words a harsh reminder for what happens when you don't. *No. He's just a kid, and he's alone. Where are his parents? Does he have parents?* Too many unanswered questions left me feeling uneasy. It was worth investigating for those questions alone.

No one was out in the area and fiddling with the door knob could send him fleeing out the back door. Shifting back on my left heel, I kicked the door right beneath the lock. It slammed against the wall revealing an empty house. No furniture in sight meant it wasn't on the short-list for any newcomers anytime soon. Which also meant he had no business being here, answering one of my questions.

The boy was nowhere in sight though there were still rooms up the steps to clear. That sixth sense in me screamed for me to halt as I made my way up the steps. Something was off. I just couldn't place what. My foot creaked under the floorboard at the top as the door to the first room peeled open. Pivoting in my approach, I allowed my instincts took over, meeting him head on. His shoulder slammed into my stomach with more weight than I'd assess him of having. I was taller and stronger though, the match was never fair to begin with. All it took was a well-timed shove, and he was on his ass.

He gave up with ease. The hopelessness in his maple colored eyes broke me. Scanning the room, I noticed a stash of food in the corner then turned back toward him. Recognition set in. I knew this face. Had been debriefed about him yesterday morning. He'd gone missing from the orphanage this week. Orphanage wasn't fair; it was more of a group home situation, but the kids there actually appeared to receive some sort of love. They'd all lost parents whether it had been on the onset of this new way of life, on the way here, or while their parents had been away on duty.

There had been some debate on whether we should search for him. I'd argued we should, as had Amaia. Jax, Prescott, and the council had been on the opposing side, however. Since he was over the age of sixteen, he was an adult in the time of an apocalypse as far as they were concerned. I couldn't blame them. He'd made it here on his own but had a hard time staying with any of his foster placements. The list of who would take kids in was short considering the way of the world, which had led him to the group home. The opposition of continuing a search had been cut down to two very simple reasons: a lack of resources and the fact that they felt he was capable of making his own decisions since he chose to run off.

I knew otherwise.

After waiting ten long years for an adoption that would never come, I knew the value of missing that familial support. I could only imagine how he was feeling now. Amaia and I had agreed to keep an eye out for him.

What would happen to him once we found him, we hadn't thought that far out. The face stared up at me with wide, panicked eyes and quickened breath answered my final sought after question of the day ...

I knew who I was. I was the man who stuck to the shadows and helped where I could. When I could.

"Abel Montgomery, we've been looking for you."

Part Four

THE HEALER & THE COWBOY

The Shot

SETH

"I'll be back, Ma." I leaned in, kissing the top of her blonde hair.

She smiled, drying off the dishes from breakfast. My father's heavy stare settled on the side of my face as he peered over the top of his book. He sat on the couch next to Uncle Harris, their deep red hair reflecting off the flames of the fireplace. Harris had been anxious the last few days. His foot tapped against the creaky wood flooring, a scowl hardened the tan lines of his face.

"Can I come?" my sister asked from the top of the steps, a cheerful grin matching the sparkle in her eyes.

I glanced between her and the rest of my family. When we were little, our cousin would drag us out of the house for the day. We'd spend the day outside playing and wandering her neighborhood. It'd been fun, always felt like an adventure of sorts. Those kinda memories couldn't be formed out on the ranch. It was always just us.

When we got older, we learned the reason for spending those countless summer days outside. Uncle Harris had ... moments when struggling with his PTSD became too much. He needed quiet some days, and having a house full of kids didn't help. Now, there were six of us in a four-bedroom house with no one to interact with but each other. Nowhere to be alone except out there.

"No," I grumbled. Family was everything to me and there was a time when I'd lost them. James's death had done a number on us. It was an accident, but that hadn't stopped his words from haunting me every day.

You better pray you get a hold on your anger, or one day you're gonna find yourself swallowed with regrets.

One slip up. One bout of anger. And I'd had to face the reality in his words. It was my fault he'd taken a hoof to the head. My fault my family had to make the decision to let James go, to come to terms that living through a tube would have made him miserable.

My father had mastered the art of quiet anger. The kind that kept you in control. His temper was short, but the way he released it was calculated. I didn't know why I was angry all the time. Just knew I was more at ease when I was out with my horses. It helped me sift through the hard shit. The guilt.

"*Yes*, you can," my mom challenged. She set a bowl

down on the counter with raised brows. "Seth, take your sister with you."

Reina had made her way down the steps, an eager smile plastered across her pale skin. I ruffled her hair as I strode by. "No can do, Ma. See you later."

I had to get out of here. Things had been tense at the house the last few days. Hunter was oddly quiet and had disappeared into our room the moment our father dismissed the table. Reina, never one to miss a beat, did her due diligence, taming the quiet with empty chatter. Our father too, though his topics had a way of silencing her.

Rounding the corner of the house, an arrow pierced the wind, skimming the side of my ear. I huffed a sigh, whirling on my boots. Reina stood on the porch, her long brown hair blowing across her reddened face. She nocked another arrow in defiance. I grinned, tossing a waved goodbye before mounting my horse and riding away.

There was something to be said about Montana air. Even in chaos, it brought peace. Helped me strengthen my weakening facade. The world around me was undisturbed, beautiful, skies so blue and vast that it shut out all the pain and suffering that lay beyond our lands. It was why I came back after James. I could run, but I couldn't hide from the love and safety I felt on our land. Without the horses I raised and the family I held dear, this was home. Always would be. Didn't need much more than that.

A hawk soared above me, unusual since the change in climate we'd faced since the world ended. The usual frigid air had caused most birds to fly south permanently. It'd been rather warm lately. Well, warm considering the weather we typically got most days. Rolling hills closed in on the open sky as I lay back on Freedom, legs dangling over his broad back as he grazed lazily on the grass in the field.

I'd hated the name my sister had given our little runaway, but it'd soon grown on me after a late night of searching for him. Reina's sing-song voice asking '*Where's our Freedom?*' as she helped me search and avoid our father's wrath at the missing stallion had been one of my core memories with her.

Our father had warned me to fix his stall for over a week since he'd first gotten out. Despite chasing after him damn near each night, fifteen-year-old me had been too hardheaded to listen. Too stubborn for my own good. Always had been. James and Hunter told me I was on my own after the second night, but not Reina. Never Reina. She always had my back, regardless our differences.

"Can I interest you in an evening hunt?" Hunter's voice broke the sound of nature as it cut into the walkie at my hip.

I reached down, unclasping it and bringing it to my lips with a smile. "Ain't that something. Came out your room with daylight to spare. With you? No thanks, better off with Reina."

"You say that like she's not the best shot in the family."

A clipped chuckle escaped me as I paused, considering my answer. "Yeah, don't let her hear you say that, though. She'll never shut up."

Reina, for as much as she yearned for the city life, was terrifyingly accurate with a bow and arrow. Since she was a six-year-old, annoying little girl tagging along on our hunts, she'd bring in the biggest game. A fact that irritated our father, expecting more from his sons. Hunter and James had always been the better brothers, refusing to hang their head in shame over the fact that their little sister had bested them. Congratulating her as if our father wasn't offering them a glare promising punishment later. It was fine. That glare meant little for them. They could get away with it. They weren't the family disappointment.

"You know what?" Hunter said. The static picked up, muffling his words. "I'll ask her instead."

Reina's sense of direction was less than impressive. Not to mention she couldn't swat off a fly without hurting herself. She couldn't fend for herself even if she wanted to. She may annoy the hell out of me, but I'd imagine a life without her would've been pretty bleak.

"Nah, I'll be back before dinner. We can leave after we eat."

Hunter's response never came. I clipped the walkie

back onto the waist of my pants, slapping the side of Freedom. The sun cast long shadows across the open field as I guided Freedom through a series of barrel maneuvers. His body was sleek, strong. Riding him felt good, like I was floating through the clouds.

The level of fluid precision we moved with as a unit gave me the false sensation that we were one. Freedom's hooves thundered against the earth from the cloverleaf pattern of barrels we weaved in and out of. Dust kicked up around us, stinging my eyes as I leaned into each turn, urging Freedom to pick up his speed. There would never be a barrel race again. The need to push for tighter turns and quicker transitions was a fruitless effort besides the pent up aggression it released for the both of us.

Freedom's muscles rippled beneath his glossy coat, his nostrils flaring as I slowed us to a gentle canter after a few intense rounds. "Good job, buddy," I murmured, gently patting his neck.

The sharp crack of gunfire echoed across the field. Birds erupted from the nearby trees, taking into a frantic flight. "Hunter?" I asked into the radio, my blood running cold.

Silence was a blessing in my life. It wasn't often I got to experience it in my home. This silence, however, was the most torturous echo of nothing. It was loud, damning. Freedom lifted his head, ears pricked forward and muscles tensed. Reluctantly, I raised the walkie again, begging for a response. "Hunter, you good, man?"

My fingers tightened around the reins. Freedom's

muscles bunched as he leaped into motion, not needing further instruction on what to do. A heart beat pounded in my ears, the throb in sync with the rhythm of hooves. It took me a moment to realize it was mine. The once serene field that lay miles away from my home blurred around me, the only focus now on reaching my family as five more shots fired into the air.

Won't Look Back

REINA

"Hurry up," Seth ordered from his room across the hall. His rifle sang through the air as he picked off straggling zombies one by one. Most had gathered outside the front door, attempting to push their way past our living room furniture.

A sob broke from my throat as I ruffled through my closet, unsure of what I needed to pack in the situation of running for my life. Hunting clothes would have to do. I stripped from my leggings and pulled on my camo pants and waterproof boots, shoving the rest of the gear on top of the canned goods I'd grabbed from the cellar.

"I'm almost done," I shouted, taking one last glance around my room both for nostalgia and to make sure I hadn't left anything important behind.

As my brother had requested, I poured gasoline in a

line from my room to his and Hunter's before slamming the door, stopping only for a moment to move their dresser and trunk to barricade us in. I grunted. The weight of the wood took a good amount of my strength. That was a good thing. Would probably buy us some time.

"I need the bag," I requested, arms full of clothes from his hunting drawer. Ammo, hunting knives and a few of his guns lined the bottom of his duffle. The food I'd grabbed would have to be enough for the both of us—at least until we could stop and search for more. *Both. Two. There are only two of us now ...*

"Leave some for Hunter in case he makes his way back."

I glanced at him warily, sliding a pistol, a round of ammo, and a can of food back into the drawer. It was pointless. Would go to waste. Zipping the bag up, I slid it back toward him, careful not to get the next line of gasoline on our belongings or splattered on our shoes.

"'Kay, Reina, I'm gonna need you to listen to me very carefully." He squinted his right eye, continuing to pick off zombies as uneven footsteps thudded down the hall. *They're closing in.* Panic began to seize my veins. "Remember how we used to watch stars on the roof as kids? We gotta climb back up there. Not a big deal. Can you do that?"

I felt my head nod, my body on autopilot. Seth motioned his head toward the window on the other side of the room, wanting me to climb out on it. He tossed me my bag of arrows for the bow in the back quiver strung across my shoulders.

"Now what?" I whispered once he appeared next to me, the door to his room thunderous as wood hit wood.

His throat cleared, turning to face me, his warm, calloused hand squeezed mine gently. "Tuck and roll. Try to land on the balls of your feet, send your bag down first. Soon as you even think your feet touch that ground, you tuck your chin and embrace the feeling of your knees coming into your chest. Let your body take control after that. It's not far, 'bout ten feet. You'll roll once, maybe twice. Then get up. Immediately."

I sniffled, dropping my bag and bow onto the flower bed beneath. I bit my lip and edged toward the end of the roof, hesitating right before making the leap.

"Reina, *now*. We have to go. I'm sorry." His voice grew impatient. We were running out of time.

Taking a deep breath, I stepped back a few feet, wanting to give myself enough grace to execute his directions as best I could. I'd never been good with athletic things. I'd rode the horses for fun, but not sport and certainly not passion the way my brothers and father had. Wasn't coordinated enough to even convince myself any sport in high school was worth going out for.

Closing my eyes, I made the jump. Foolishly deciding to let my body tell me when to tuck my chin instead of watching to see when my feet would connect. The impact forced my eyes open, barely seeing Seth take his turn as the world passed me in a flurry. A shooting pain soared up my ankle and leg, ceasing only from the distraction of my head slamming into the ground on the second roll. The world spun, sheer willpower bringing me to my feet as instructed.

Slowly, I turned to my brother. His focus shifted between reloading his gun and the sides of the house. No zombies over here. Yet. My eyes found the window we'd leaped from seconds before. Even from here, I could see his room was now filled with them; their attention not yet outside on the ground. A lighter flicked at my side, drawing my curiosity back toward my brother.

A piece of cloth hung from his mouth, his teeth clenched, tearing it apart. "We need to go get the horses," he mumbled. "My guns are of no use—they'll only attract more out to us in the back of the house. I'm going to wrap this around your arrow and light it. I need you to hit somewhere inside my room."

My vision blurred at the thought of burning down the only home we'd ever known. Our father had ever known. I'd been so consumed by the panic and the chaos of the last few hours that Seth's request to pour a trail of gas throughout the house had barely registered. I'd simply listened without a second thought. This morning we'd had breakfast as a family. We laughed over homemade biscuits and jam and went about our day. Our father, our mother, Uncle Harris, Hunter, Seth.

A family of six was down to two in a matter of hours.

When I awoke this morning, shivering from the draft entering my room and snuggling close to my weighted blanket, I'd not imagined I'd twice now be asked to pull a trigger I had no desire to pull. My arms shook. Bow wavering and lip trembling as I tried to do what I was asked. There would be no cost I wouldn't pay to keep my last family member alive. Willing to do whatever I was asked to keep my brother safe and his temper under control, though it appeared that I was the one that needed help.

Seth came up behind me, lowered my bow, and took it from my unsteady grasp. I turned my back, not wanting to watch. The sound of my bow snapped and the loud cracking noise of wood roared. Flame took over his childhood bedroom, the screeching sound of the creatures burning muted below the blaze.

His hands clamped down on my shoulders, guiding me toward the stables. He stopped before The Duke, his first horse, weighing his options. Seth hesitated as he kept moving toward Freedom. The Duke was old. Without knowing where we were headed, taking him along would be a massive risk.

"We should let the others loose," I said, stopping to rub The Duke gently on the nose. "At least give them a shot at life."

He nodded his head in agreement. "Good idea." Turning his back to me, he strode toward Hunter's horse, Daisy's stable, patting her gently before opening the gate.

One by one, he approached each horse calmly, careful not to spook them, offering a treat as a peace offering. With each open gate, Seth led them toward the opening, patting them on the hind end and encouraging them to go free. A shudder went through his body as he watched The Duke ride off. He loved his horses, probably more than he loved me.

I saddled up my mare, pretending I couldn't hear the crackling flames consuming our house in the distance. Making sure my weapons and bags were secured, I steered the large Arabian out of the stables, trotting up next to Seth.

"Let's go," he said, riding away without glancing back.

If he won't look back, then neither will I. Following my brother's lead, I took a deep breath and left it all behind.

We rode for miles; the plains giving way to tree lines and back to plains. The mountain our ranch lay at the base of was long gone on the horizon. Silent tears streamed down my face. The clothes on our backs, our horses, and what I'd managed to gather in our packs were the only possessions we had left.

Everything I loved or cared about was left behind, nothing but a pummel of ash. I thought of James, the brother I'd connected to the most now left behind, without even a farewell. His grave was underneath a tree, acres back on our property. Our mother—left in the yard unburied. Uncle Harris and our father too. And Hunter.

Hunter would never find peace.

My family had finally felt complete, united again after James's death years before the world had come to an end. His death had destroyed Seth. Caused him to leave and further torn our family apart at the loss of yet another son.

It had been his fault. We'd danced around it, but it was true, and ultimately the reason no one had fought his departure.

If he hadn't let his temper get the best of him, he'd have thought better of falling victim to a fit of rage—coming into the stables, slamming objects around had spooked the horse James was tending to. The impact of his horse's hoof had fractured James' skull.

After months of no brain activity, our parents had made the best call they could make. My brother had been full of life. Finding joy in taking risks and relishing at the idea of spending a life outdoors. He wouldn't have wanted to live. Not like that.

Seth had taken off the very next day. Moving from our ranch to work on a friend's ranch out in Idaho. The guilt ate away at him, but what we hadn't realized was that he'd sought out help. James had always told him he was too smart to let anger ruin his life, so Seth had wanted to change. To stop being an angry and temperamental person and put the past behind him.

He'd returned to the ranch shortly before things went south. Months later—once the dust had settled—things had begun to feel as they had when I was a child.

Things would never be that way again.

Lost in thought, I jolted as Seth pulled the reins on my horse. My mare and his stallion were now side by side.

"Reina, enough. Hey, it's time to stop for the night." His voice was even, but his eyes were rimmed red and the color had drained from his tanned face. I glanced around, taking in the scene before me. We'd stopped outside a cabin in the middle of nowhere, trees the only landscape visible to the eye. "I'll go in, clear it. Make sure it's safe."

"No," I said firmly, his head whipping back in my direction. "I'll come too."

The eyes so similar to my own trailed me up and down, assessing my condition, brow scrunched. Pleased by whatever he saw, he answered, "Together."

Once the house was cleared, he offered up the couch, opting to keep first watch from the chair in front of the only window. It was a simple hunter's cabin and there was only one exit. I felt his eyes studying me in the dark, even with my eyes closed.

"You might as well say what's on your mind," I said, my usual patience lost in my exhaustion.

He cleared his throat, shifting in his seat. "You sure Hunter didn't slip into one of the sheds? Wait out the herd? If he left without a weapon, then there's a chance he didn't know how bad the situation was until he saw the smoke from the house."

There were sheds placed randomly throughout the property. An attempt to lessen the number of trips we'd have to take back and forth for materials and in case of emergencies or waiting out bad weather.

Positive. I cleared my throat. "Yes." My lie had been elaborate enough. To go further in-depth would make things ... complicated.

"We should go back in the morning."

No. Familiar panic rose in the form of bile in my

throat. "Go back to what? A burned down house with momma in the yard? See if daddy turned or if the water had left Uncle Harris's lungs? There's nothing there for us anymore, Seth."

The outline of his body stiffened, suspicious with the harshness of my words. His hands tapped angrily against the window frame, but he said nothing else for the rest of the night. I turned. Pushing my face into the cushions of the couch, I closed my eyes in an attempt to force myself to sleep. The thought of my new reality caused me to toss and turn.

My entire life, I'd been the odd one out in the family. Had loved the ranch and wondrous adventures I'd grown up having, but had always wanted more. And now I was going to get it. Problem was, it had become a world I no longer knew anything about. A world that scared me, full of death and darkness. I wasn't sure I'd survive in a world like that.

Now it was just me and Seth. A brother who I'd spend the rest of my life harboring a dark secret from. I'd never been good with secrets. But I'd try for him.

If the cost of his happiness was my truth, I'd forever live a lie.

No Matter The Costs

SETH

What do you do when you know the person you trust the most in the world is lying through their teeth? I knew my sister. Over the two decades of her life, she'd been nothing shy of a terrible liar. The issue I found myself having on hand was what exactly she was lying about.

A good liar lies through omission, while a great liar will sprinkle in small truths.

I'd never gotten away with much as a kid. Our father had a way of knowing my tells. I don't know what haunted her most nights these passing months, but I was damn scared to find out. Family was everything to me, and Reina was the final thread left hanging.

Trust is a fickle thing.

A lifetime to build and only a moment to disappear. It

was why I refused to let my mind wander to such a place that would make me question her. Reina had a good soul —it was what everyone loved about her. Surely if she had chosen to keep things to herself, there'd been a good reason to do so.

So I refused to pry my nose where it didn't belong. Perhaps she was protecting herself and her own mental being. She was my sister, and keeping her safe was my responsibility. I couldn't do that if my questioning sent her into a frantic spiral. Her emotions had been all over the place as of late. Asking the wrong question on the wrong day had resulted in weeks of setbacks heading back north. It would be better this way—to let her work through whatever happened back home at her own pace.

Still, I couldn't help but wonder what had happened to our family. To our home. Giving up on Hunter being okay meant giving up on our family. I felt him out there, knew in my soul he was alright. A twin would know if their other half was gone. That's what people always said, *right?* Hunter was tough as nails. A skilled outdoors man. Surely he'd made his way northeast as planned.

A creak sounded on the wooden steps of a long abandoned cabin we'd found on a back road. With the boarded-up windows, I couldn't see shit outside, but the horses were quiet. I peered back at Reina still asleep on the couch, brushing off the noise as mother nature at work. Having enhanced senses had its perks, but I would never miss the quiet of the past. Before my body had changed, before I could hear everything from everyone and everywhere. At least listening to the inner thoughts of the surrounding people took significant effort. It was hard to do without people sensing I was there. It'd been a shock when it first happened, a shout within Reina's mind when I'd thought the worst had happened and she'd answered back.

A storm was brewing. The wind had picked up on the ride here. There was a chance it would pass over. If not, then we'd be stuck here for God knew how long. With only the supplies we'd managed to frantically toss in a pack, we'd taken advantage of the world around us before depleting our resources. When dawn broke, I'd have to check on the traps before Reina woke up.

The horses shuffled near the tree we'd tied them to for the night. I stiffened, listening for any disturbance in the area. Before things had changed, our father had taught us to use the forest as a tell for danger. If the world went silent, then it was time to get the hell out. That wasn't the case anymore. The colder it got, the fewer critters and nature we found around.

Still, I could listen for the trees. A snapping of a twig. Maybe the bristling of leaves. Or the clicks and groans of the decaying remains of what were once people. My fingers clamped around the barrel of my gun. We were down to our last rounds of ammo. Even with the conservative use of what we had, it hadn't last us long at all. One would have thought such a commodity would be easy to find around these parts. It appeared everyone else had thought the same. While food and clothing were plenty to find and left for the next, weapons were not.

A higher-pitched groan came from the east of the cabin near the horses. They whinnied with fear. Glancing at my still sleeping sister, I pushed to my feet and made my way to the door. Two zombies were on me at the quiet clasp of the door. They latched down with their teeth, finding nothing but hide and layers of fur to clamp onto. The hunger in their movements shook the rifle from my hand.

Pain seared through my head as their uncoordinated weight slammed me into the door, my temple exploding with flashes of white stars. The door opened, Reina's terrified scream on the other side. Attention on me was abandoned as zombies entered the room. There were more than I initially assessed, following after my sister. Reina scrambled behind the couch, searching for one of the few arrows she'd carved out until falling victim to sleep. They were on her before she had a chance.

A hard, cold body fell atop me. I pushed up in an attempt to create some distance. Shrill screams rang out from across the room. Terrified. My sister sounded terrified, but it went further than that. Her cry for help was filled with the dread of death. And I'd be damned if that happened under my watch.

Kicking out, my boot collided with the chest of the zombie still trying to claw its way through my face. It reared into the wall with a thud. The hard impact did nothing to stop it from resetting for another attack. I glanced around the room for a weapon. Anything I could use to my benefit. Locking onto the lamp on the table next to the couch, I swung down. Sticky, tar colored blood splattered across my face at the connection to its skull.

Its body dragged with the effort it took to pull free from its head. Reina's panicked, tear-filled stare met mine in between the heads of three remaining zombies. She shook her hands to find no relief. Her magic would not answer her call. When I lost sight of her under the zombies, the only thing I saw was red and black.

Launching myself at the undead, I grabbed the nearest one's head and twisted with full force. Its bones crunched under my grip. With a fierce slam, I drove its head into the wall and watched as it crumpled with a lifeless thud.

"Behind me, Reina." I offered a hand to my sister, who stared up at me with wide blue eyes. Moore eyes. Possibly the only Moore left. "I got you."

My sister straightened against the blood stained wall, her hands trembling as she passed an arrow to me. I took it, my hands slick with gore, and aimed for the eye socket of the next zombie. It broke with the pull out and left me defenseless against the final one gnawing in our direction. My fists pounded into rotting, cold gray flesh. Rage surged through my veins—a searing, stinging feeling that was all too familiar. I would protect my sister, no matter the costs.

Pinky

REINA

"Easy, breathe."

I huffed in annoyance. "I could close my eyes and make this shot." We'd spent the last week making our way through Yellowstone. Headed nowhere yet somewhere at the same time.

"I know, but something about how easy it is to piss you off made me want to comment, anyway."

His husky laugh made me grin from ear to ear. I kept my eyes on my brother as I fired, the deer three-hundred yards away going down silently and I winked. The past few months on the road had brought us closer than ever. We'd had no choice but to trust each other blindly, putting the fate of the other into each other's hands. He'd saved me more times than I could count, and I'd saved him a few times myself—though he'd never admit it out loud.

We made a quick fire, cooking the meat to a safe temperature, then took off. Never staying in one spot too long made sure we gave ourselves enough time to get out of dodge and find another place to eat and sleep. I'd taken to dousing our fire pit with my water magic, wanting to keep the remnants of a cooked meal and signs of life minimal. It'd come in handy back on the ranch once I'd accepted it wasn't an accident and no, I wasn't hallucinating. I still lacked control with my gifts—I could either douse things slightly and take forever to do so, or create a potential flash flood. There was no in between.

Seth's hide poncho brushed against my shoulder, providing extra warmth and encouraging me to scoot closer in the depths of the cave. There hadn't been any cabins nearby, which didn't matter much since it'd only make us a target out in Yellowstone. A feral scream rang out, followed by the sound of what was surely someone dying. It was close. Not directly in front of our cave, but close enough to hear them being ripped to pieces. *Alive.*

"Do you remember that time James convinced you that you were adopted?" He wrapped his arm around my body, pulling me closer.

I peered up at him, taking the bait and offering a huffed laugh. "Yeah. I literally cried so loud mom came out in a towel, pissed. She could hear the commotion from the shower. Hadn't even washed all Nessie's birthing gook out of her hair yet."

One of the horses had gone into labor that morning.

The birth had been difficult, but she'd managed to save both the momma and her calf.

"She looked like a damn zombie herself," Seth teased.

Silent laughs shook our bodies at the memory.

"Hunter was *livid* when he got home from the fair."

He nodded his head, the movement pulling at the strands of my hair. "Well, if you were adopted, then that meant he was too." Silence took back over at the thought.

Hunter and I didn't resemble the rest of our family. We'd all shared our father's eyes, but Seth and James had taken after our father and his red hair. Our mother's kind eyes were brown, glimmering, resembling pieces of gold against her tan skin and blonde hair. Hunter and I favored our maternal grandfather. The Italian blood ran victorious against the Irish. Our dark features stood out against our pale skin and bright eyes.

A warm droplet fell against my forehead. I ignored it, letting him feel as though he was making me strong, but knowing I was simply adding to it. I'd realized that I had an additional gift once it became a bit *too* easy to talk him down during fits of rage over the past few months.

The journey had been far from complicated, but there had been several situations that were tough to get ourselves out of. That added on to time spent lost, and having nowhere to go ... the anger had been justified. Nevertheless, unhelpful.

"We should try heading north now," he said, breaking the silence.

"Newport's only eleven days from here."

His body jerked at the words. "That's where we've been headed?"

Newport was a small coastal town in Oregon. Our mother had grown up there and we'd visited during the holidays while our grandparents were still alive. We hadn't been back in years, but it was the perfect size to pass through with limited risk. Our mother's reluctance to sell our grandparents' house was only an added plus to provide us a nice place to recover.

I tensed, not wanting to trigger him, quietly pushing my power out to calm him. "I think it's where we should head. I met a girl at the river a few days ago. She said that part of the country is done. All of it. If it wasn't the undead, the weather would freeze out the rest."

Seth stared out into the dark void beyond the cave entrance. Minutes passed, yet he said nothing. I closed my eyes, pretending to rest as I worked to force more of my power out. It was dark here, but his own heightened abilities made it where he could see just enough to spot my lie. A shiver went through his body, not yet knowing about the extra gift I possessed.

That's how I viewed them, as gifts. I wasn't sure how they worked, or if they could be felt or go undetected. It wasn't uncommon to run into others, my story was believable enough, but still caused pause, hesitation. It was a Hail Mary; I needed to give more, say more, to dissuade him.

There was nothing left for us up north, no family that would be waiting. At least none worth fleeing to. None that I could be sure wouldn't lead my brother down a dark path he'd fall easy prey to. Our cousin could be rather ... convincing. The similarities between her and Seth would cause nothing but trouble and questions they'd ensure they found answers to. Their relentless energy would be damning, and I wasn't quite sure I wanted to know definitively that it was really only the two of us left. Couldn't take that. Sometimes no answers are the best answers for everyone.

"It's gotten cold, Seth. Even with the gear we've managed to get, it's too cold to make it there safely. Let's wait out the winter." I shrugged. "Try again in the spring and hit the coast for a bit. At least we know the area, and if there's people, maybe they'll know something about the state of things up north."

We wouldn't. I knew that, but if it helped convince him, then to hell with it.

Minutes later, he turned away. "No later than spring, Reina."

"Pinky," I said. Cursing myself for making a promise I never intended to keep.

RESPONSIBILITIES

SETH

I WANTED TO GO HOME. THIS LIFE, OUT ON THE road, stuck inside enclosed spaces and shimmying among the outskirts of abandoned homes and cities was not the life I'd been hoping to lead. There is peace in the fresh, open air. Now all there was, was death. The smell of death. The sounds of death. The actions ... the *need* to cause death.

From animals. From zombies. From people.

That was what took the largest toll. I wasn't built for this. Losing James had nearly stolen my own life. Having to take more in order to ensure Reina and I were safe was an action I don't think I'd ever like to get used to. People were sick. They'd lost their values, their morals, and their way long before we'd ever had to flee the ranch. Godless savages. Life had become kill or be killed. I don't think that was ever going to change again. Not in my lifetime.

When the weather cleared and the storms slowed down, we could finally make our way back north. Reina's reluctance to head home made me hesitant. Something wasn't right. I did my best not to push her, she'd never done well under pressure. Since she was a kid she'd talked about walking away and leaving the ranch, but this was different. She'd changed. It seemed less about what up north had to offer and more about running away from her life's problems. Her problems were my problems now, she was my responsibility. I just wished she'd trust I was capable of taking care of us both.

Instead she was full of opinions and constantly putting her foot down on any sort of guidance I offered. I would follow my sister anywhere—that was indisputable. She was all I had left. So I bode my time, stopped fighting her and waited for the right moment to try to steer us in the right direction. My sister was stubborn, but she was also smart. She was right, we didn't have the proper resources we needed to make the journey. Not in the current climate.

If there was one thing our father had instilled in us, it was to always be prepared. Without proper preparation, you were as good as dead. That's how I knew Hunter was okay. He was out there, somewhere, probably doing his best to make his way to us as planned.

So I'd wait. One day the opportunity would present

itself for a safe journey to be made. I'd get us there. Together, that was where what was left of my family belonged. There was no place to call home without them.

My Brother's Keeper

REINA

I'm a liar. A manipulator. A fake. A phony.

I am my brother's keeper.

It was my week to navigate, he'd trusted me to guide us to Newport. To get us safely to the coast. And I did get us to the coast at least. I'd avoided all road signs, told him we were taking the quickest route, that I'd double checked and even wrongly pointed to random markers on our map.

He had trusted me, and now we were too far south to make the journey safely. We didn't have much ammo left, even with me forging my own bows. The powers I possessed were practically useless. *I* was useless without knowing how to wield them to our advantage.

He hadn't said the words, but I could see it in his eyes every time we took a moment for me to practice, once we were able to confirm we were alone. We'd been lingering near the border of California, when Seth had heard of a place where we could work and recover. Excitement consumed him at the thought of gathering enough material and ammo to make it back north and reunite with family long-lost to us. Reluctantly, I'd agreed with hopes he'd change his mind. The settlement itself seemed fine from what he'd described; things couldn't be much worse than being on the road for weeks at a time.

Metal walls towered over us, the gate squeaking as it opened and a handsome brown-skinned boy with locs stood in front, arms crossed as he took us in. I blushed under the intensity of his gaze, suddenly feeling embarrassed of my appearance, especially when he looked so clean. All six of the guards at the gate did, actually. And Seth and I were the embodiment of ... savages.

Not just savages. Like Children of the Corn from the fields with our torn hunting gear we'd rotated into our daily apparel for months. The heavy coats we'd acquired while traveling were now crunched into one of the packs on the back of my mare, no longer needed under the suffocating heat on the coast.

"You have to dismount," the man said, holding out a hand to help me off my horse.

"Why?" Seth said more aggressively than necessary. "My horses stay with me."

His locs shook around his head, eyes scanning Seth before dismissing him and turning back toward me. "I'm sure you can understand my orders. Why I can't let people we don't know have access beyond this gate with an animal capable of hitting speeds of what? Sixty? Seventy miles an hour?"

I did, and it made sense. Taking his hand, I allowed him to assist me, though it wasn't needed. "You'll have to forgive him. We've been on our own for ... some time now. Before that, just with our family on a ranch. *Manners* isn't a familiar word to him." The man was tall, not as tall as my brother, but tall enough that he still had a few inches over me. Not as rare these days as the ones before.

"Reina," Seth growled, not liking all the information I was disclosing, but I was nervous, rambling and excited.

I changed gears as I grabbed my bags, ready to bring them in with us. "This some kind of militia or something?"

"Something of the sort, a bit less organized, but yeah. First line of defense for The Compound," he answered. His dark brown eyes were shifty, but trustworthy. Aware.

The gates opened wide, and I was transported into another world. *The Compound.* Fighting against a smile large enough to make my cheeks ache, I walked forward, knowing me entering would be the only thing to get Seth off his horse. Needing to follow me in and make sure I was safe or the guilt would eat him alive.

The man stopped in front of me, cutting off my path and pointed at my bags. "We'll have to take those, unfortunately. Until a final decision is made. You'll get everything inside back, but, safety first, so ..."

"You wanna take our stuff?" I questioned, fist

clenching my bow, defensiveness creeping in over trusting the last things I owned to a stranger.

He nodded, reading my thoughts. "You'll get them back. Don't worry. If you miss something, you can tell her Riley took your stuff." He winked, motioning to grab my stuff. I handed them over hesitantly, not knowing who the 'she' was I was meant to talk to or what a final decision meant.

Another guard walked up, ready to grab my belongings, but was shook off. "I got it. Mohammed, can you please take my new friend Reina and her ... brother?" he questioned, and I nodded in response. "To intake. I'll let them know we have new arrivals and have these checked. They'll be waiting for you wherever you end up. Good luck," he said, before walking off.

My gut churned. *Good luck?* I wished I could have at least washed off, worn cleaner clothes, maybe brushed my hair or something. First impressions were everything, especially in moments like this. Looking like a savage was probably a sure indicator that you were one. In today's world, judging a book by its cover could be the difference between life or death.

Though our journey had been easy compared to most, the weather and our own grief had been our biggest obstacles. Still, we'd done things to survive. We'd killed people. Seth had killed people, and I had at least stopped us in our tracks, demanded we'd buried them. We had to. It was either them or us. And I would do anything to make sure it would always be us, forever. But this place could be a new start for us both.

I frowned at him, every inch of his demeanor lethal. Threatening. I pushed my powers out, sending him a sense of peace. Wanting his mind to be open to the possibility of calling it home. Each area we passed through was designed differently than the last. There weren't many buildings; in fact, most of the walled area was still a rubble mess. But the parts that were built were brilliant.

The cobblestone pathways flowed through The Compound, remnants of different cultures and time periods stamped into each completed structure. Victorian. Gothic. Tuscany. Modern. What should be a mess felt like its own journey. A guide through the lives of the people who inhabited the settlement, each bringing a piece of home with them. Their own bit of happiness, as simple as it sounded. It was the most beautiful place I'd had the grace of walking.

I never wanted to leave.

"General Living Quarters," Mohammed said. "You'll probably end up a street or two over."

I smiled at him, nodding as I took it all in. "We get our own house?"

"Reina."

Mohammed dropped a brow as he took in my brother's snarl. "You can stay where you want, really. It's mainly a roommate system. We're pretty communal around here. Best I can say is you might get lucky and it'll be a minute before you get a roommate. There are a few houses with only a room or two, but those are pretty high in demand, kept for families with a kid or two."

The scent of fresh bread wafted through the air as we rounded a corner to a large brick building. My mouth watered at the promise of real food. God, it had been so long I'd eaten something I didn't have to hunt, gather, or kill to keep.

We entered the building, cool from the outside heat. The first moment of reprieve in a long time. Mohammed dropped us into a homey room, nodding before closing us in behind the wooden door. The room smelled of dust, eucalyptus, and a hint of coffee. A wide smile covered my face at the decor, my eyes meeting Seth and faltering. He held my stare, undoubtedly deciding on how to tell me that he'd changed his mind, no longer wanting to stay. The door opened, and a doe-eyed woman a few years older than myself walked in.

Her clothes were clean, fit to respond to any situation, but relatively normal. The curls danced around her narrow shoulders against her reddish-brown skin. She was healthy, the smile on her face beautiful. Power emanated from her, confidence seeping from her movements though she hadn't yet spoken. My face and neck warm again as she took me in.

She was the type of woman I'd always dreamed of settling down with. An auburn-haired man strolled in after her; her hair bounced as she intently studied his face, the smile pushing at her lips saying everything about the tension between them.

"Welcome to Monterey," he said, noticing my stare. Irish, *huh*. I hadn't expected the accent.

"I'm Amaia," the woman said, her raspy voice strong but welcoming. "This is Jax. We'll be conducting your intake interview today."

She reached her hand out, Seth and I both staring at it. Uncertain how to interact with others anymore. Amaia smiled, taking a seat and not appearing insulted at all.

Jax hovered for a moment. "You two look like you've been through a lot. Can we get you anything before we start?"

I shook my head, Seth glared in response. Jax took his seat. "It's okay to be nervous. The Compound can be a bit overwhelming at times, especially with all the construc-tion going on."

"What kinda interview?" Seth interrupted, tone harsh.

A soft smile pulled at Amaia's round lips. "Sounds more invasive than what it is. Just want to get to know you a bit better, ask the things that matter. Make sure it's a good fit."

"A fit for what?" I asked, curiosity taking over.

"There's over ten thousand people here," Jax offered, leaning forward. "A place for everyone if you know where to look."

Ten thousand. Wow. Even before the world ended, I'd never been around that many people at once. Vacationing wasn't really our thing unless it was Newport or visiting family up north. I'd dreamed of moving to the city, honestly, even a decently sized town, but had never considered it a real possibility until now.

If there was a place for everyone, then that meant 'a good fit' was polite words for 'not a psychopathic killer.' I glared at Seth, squeezing his hand and begging him to play along. His face contorted in something of a sneer, as close to a smile as I would get. I'd lost my brother the second I'd hopped off my horse and walked through these gates, but I didn't care. He was safe here, would always be safe here from the look of things.

Amaia studied us both, taking a deep breath before tucking the paperwork into a drawer.

"Let's scrap the interview. We can chat. Just the four of us. Come on, fire away." She winked. "Ask any questions you have. I think you're going to like what we have to offer."

Part Five

THE SEER

Wrath

TOMOE

I'd awoken not to noise, but a vision.

My family was sitting around the coffee table in the living room wearing the same clothing from when I'd decided to call it a night and head to bed. A makeshift gag stuffed my mother's mouth, her cries lost behind the cloth. My sisters rocked back and forth, wiggling beneath the ties that were now secured around their ankles and wrists.

Crashing came from the kitchen. There were people in there, raiding through our food, medicine, and cutlery.

"Is there anyone else in this house?" a booming voice asked, face out of view.

"No," my father said, his tone firm, giving nothing away.

A yelp sounded to my right, and my head turned. The man at the edge of my sight was ordinary looking, but a *permanent cruel snarl appeared across his filthy face. My little sister crunched over, gasping for air, her forehead taking on the weight of her body.*

I'm speaking, except I'm not. "No. There's no one else here." *The voice is small but fierce.* "It's just us. There's no one else."

My sister Kana. It was a lie. *I'm here.* I'd gone to bed early that night, not feeling well and leaving my family to finish playing board games. Something we'd done much of as of late.

The scene changed. *My sisters were being dragged from the house. The living room was a mess, lost to the chaos of a good fight. Kana glanced around the room, making sure she'd take in every detail.* An addition to the long list of secrets the two of us developed. That explained the vividness of my vision. I'd never had one this clear before. They were usually only small glimpses of an interaction never lasting more than a few seconds.

To my horror, this one lasted minutes. *Our father was yelling, screaming for the men to not take his girls.* My sisters were not defenseless. They had learned to defend themselves through martial arts as children. They would not go easily.

"No! No!" my father pleaded, the man's boots driving into his ribs. A loud crack sounded over the mayhem as he buckled over.

My mother was on her side, trying to wiggle her way toward my sisters. Her efforts futile and words caught on the cloth still placed into her mouth.

I sat up in bed with a gasp, coming too. "Damnit," I muttered, cursing myself for not having any weapons in my room.

Poor planning on my part. My grandfather's katana would have to do. I'd practiced with it many times for fun, but never intended to use it as a weapon. Wasn't sure how it'd hold up.

It was well made. He'd crafted it as a young boy, taught by his own father, who'd been taught by his own. It was then passed down to my father, who, in turn, passed it to me. I wasn't the oldest, or the youngest. But I'd shown the most interest. Asked the most questions as a kid, wanting to document my family's history in my journal.

I slipped off my socks, not wanting them to be a disadvantage against the wood floors throughout my family home. Light on the balls of my feet, I closed the door to my room and crept down the hallway. I froze, startled as someone turned the corner. The shock on his face matched my own as I forced myself to focus, eyes scanning his body for any weapons. He had none within reach. None of that mattered. A knife would be nothing against the length of my katana. I swung without a second thought, his head falling to the floor before he could muster a warning to any others.

Yeah, this will do just fine.

Downstairs was quiet. Too quiet for anyone to be putting up a fight anything close to what I'd seen in my vision. The tang of iron hit my nostrils as my feet hit the last step, and I rounded the corner. *Too late.* I'd been too late. Two strange men stood over my sister's bodies, dragging them like dismembered mannequins after a holiday sale.

What was once the side of Kana's beautiful face, was now nothing more than a clump of exposed muscles. Three undead pieces of shit lay sprawled off to the side, knives through their skulls. The stillness of my body and shadows in the downstairs hallway helped me avoid detection as the men made their way out the front door. I'd deal with them later.

Rustling came from the kitchen. Another set of men made their way into the living room, arms full of food, and my mother's jarred tea. *Idiots*. I'd bet my life on their assumption of it being some sort of ale in its dark coloring. Their shirts were covered in dark blood, faces ashen, remnants of fear in every step they took. They were jumpy. On edge as they kept peering over their shoulders toward the back door. *Open*. This had been unplanned. Unexpected.

My vision from earlier had changed as quickly as it had arrived. Fate having other ideas on how my family would meet their end. The undead had entered through the backdoor, foolishly left open from these assholes' own intrusion. Diverting their plans and ruining my chances of saving my family.

I glanced back at their waistlines—knives again. No guns. My reach would be further than theirs, but I was outnumbered. I'd have to be both silent and quick. I could be quiet, but I wasn't sure I was capable of being quick. I could fight, yes. A damn good fighter too, but this ... this was new. My family had been cooped up in our home since the world had ended many moons ago. We went out when we had to, but for the most part had managed to get by with minimal confrontation.

They stepped over something on the floor. My eyes shot to the ground, following their movements. On the ground, my father lay in a pool of blood, slumped atop my mother with part of his neck absent. Her eyes wide, as if she'd seen their final moment coming. Even tied up, my father's last efforts were to protect my mother.

I charged forward and lost myself to blind fury.

My katana swung through the necks of the men, not letting them get close enough to grab or stab at me. One lost his hand in the process, forcing the others who fled my parents' room at the commotion to attempt to tackle me, lunging and limbs flailing wildly. *Untrained.*

I regained control outside. Rain slicked my hair flat against my skull as I stumbled over Kana's crumpled body, hand on my other sister's—June—stomach, wanting to cover the bite marks that now exposed her intestines. The smooth porcelain skin no more.

I removed my hand as I wished Kana peace into the next life, not wanting to drag June into the unknown. Kana and I had been treading a *very* thin line. The idea of possessing unknown magic intriguing us, sending us down a rabbit hole to learn more. Obtain all the knowledge we could, a dance with darkness. Except it wasn't dark. Not to us. It brought us comfort. Brought us peace.

"Earth to earth, ashes to ashes, dust to dust; in the sure and certain hope of rebirth," I said, using my blade to make a small cut on my palm to drop over Kana's body.

Short on time and unsure if they had more men headed our way, I made my way inside. Desperate to honor my sister properly, I stepped over the dead to gather the candles from the living room. There was no accelerant. We hadn't needed any with my family all possessing fire in their veins.

My sister would not get the burial or cremation she deserved. None of them would. Placing the candles around her body, I sniffled, pulling a lighter from my pocket and leaning it close to the sleeve of her shirt.

A soft whimper sounded over the rain. In a meditative state, I walked a few feet away. Taking my time, ensuring the last few moments of his life were spent in excruciating pain. Wanting him to know that he'd begged for his life to no avail.

"Please ... help. I'm ... I'm sorry," the last of the band of thieves said, wincing under the weight of my bare foot now pressed into his ribs. "I didn't wanna come. They made—"

"You should be," I said.

Letting Wrath guide me, his head rolled.

Change

TOMOE

Pointless. Everything now was pointless. Aimlessly wandering around by myself, no longer moving with purpose. Desire.

I'd fled my family home over a year ago, running off anger and adrenaline. Set out to find the group those disgusting excuses for men had come from, with no luck. No number of prayers, worship, or offerings had given me answers. Maybe the lack of answers *was* answer enough. The men had moved without training or structure. It was possible it was just a group of assholes hoping to score that had wanted my sisters for some nefarious reason and not a larger plan.

That was life now. It was the reason I'd chosen to stay away from larger groups, had watched the same situation occur from the shadows, stepping in when I could. Ending the worthless little lives of walking pieces of shit.

Then war had broken out and the crappy world I found myself living in became darker. Colder. There wasn't much left for people to hang onto these days. Humanity was on the brink of falling.

War ruined what humanity most had left. The moral code we'd all clung to no longer existed. At least not in any places I'd wandered through since the war had ended.

Transient Nation was okay. Set up for people like me. People who didn't want to exist without some sort of common law or rule, but didn't want to settle in the confines of a city after watching the world crumble the way it had before. New Mexico was hotter than hell itself, which meant not too many people wanted to travel through it on foot. The place was barren in both population and landscape, the way I preferred.

My carelessness caught up to me on a simple food run. Accustomed to the schedules of the few who'd set up camp in the area, I'd decided to cut between buildings, wanting to avoid any interactions. Tunnel-visioned on sticking to the shadows, I hadn't accounted for what may have once been attached to the walls.

A nail scraped against my side, breaking the skin and caused me to hiss in pain. I didn't stop. Didn't think about the cut again until the swelling started hours later. By the time I'd realized I needed to search for alcohol to cleanse it, I'd already succumbed to the confusion of infection. The layout of the house I was squatting in no longer made sense as I felt my way toward the street. At the second storefront, my breathing turned rapid, my body cold and clammy despite the heat of the day.

I didn't make it to the next store.

I was lucky. A family had found me dying in the streets and decided that they couldn't leave me there on the brink of death.

"Let me out!" I'd screamed, ramming into the bedroom to no avail. It didn't budge. I felt myself hyperventilating, taking in my surroundings and finding nothing but a bed and dresser surrounding me in the piss-colored room that smelled of dust and mold.

The soothing voice of a woman came through the door. "I'm going to open the door now, but I need you to take a step back and remain calm." A breath caught in my throat as I hesitated. "We found you nearly dying on the streets of Santa Fe. I'll explain everything—just. Please calm down, you're scaring the kids."

Indeed, there were stifled cries in the background.

"We?" I asked through the door, not missing a beat and doubting a woman and small children could get by on their own now. Not without a small arsenal.

"Yes. My husband and our kids."

My vision blurred, and my heart pulsed. Pacing the room, I searched for another exit. Finding none but the window that was currently barred. *No escape.* I had no intention of being in an enclosed space with any man. Not after the men at my house. Not after the things I'd seen out on the road.

"Just you," I whispered, unsure if she could hear my plea. "Please."

There was shuffling beyond the door before the woman cleared her throat. "Sure. Just me."

Taking a deep breath, I focused on grounding myself. Wanting to be clear minded for whatever came next.

Stepping back from the door, I answered her request. "I'm away."

The door creaked open. A man with a gun on the other side of the crack met my stare. I ran forward, slamming my body into the door once more, chest heaving. Shame fell upon me at my cowardice. My family would be ashamed of my lack of courage. They'd stood proudly and without fear in their own deaths. Yet here I was ...

"No. No, it's okay. He's not going to hurt you. It's just me coming in." She pushed on when I offered no response. "I'm not going to hurt you either."

The room remained silent aside from the sound of my quick, panicked breaths.

"He only wants to make sure I'm safe. We don't ... we don't know you. Anything about you, but we saved you. There are worse things we could have done. We chose to save you instead. And now we need to make sure you're safe to let out. At least while our kids are here."

I pondered her words for a moment. "Where's my katana?"

"You can have it back. After we talk."

Slowly, I opened the door. A woman walked in, her

face harsh and worn with exhaustion, but her voice was kind. A teacher's voice.

"I'm Laurel," she said. "I'd say nice to meet you, but the circumstances we meet under aren't exactly pleasant. Are they?"

Her hand extended toward mine and I stepped back. My backside now pressed against the barred window. *And why exactly do you think they are barred, Tomoe?* I asked myself, letting my mind wander to the worst-case scenario.

"House came that way. Wasn't exactly the nicest neighborhood before all this mess, but when you're on the road all the time, shelter is shelter. What's your name?" Observant and direct. *Duly noted.*

"Tomoe."

"Well, Tomoe, let me fill you in on what you've missed."

The door had been locked for their own safety. They didn't know me and had small kids in the house, but her motherly instinct had prevented her from walking past my body that day. Not wanting me to be left out there on my own, an easy victim to the next passerby. She knew what it was like to be a woman in this world of ours.

Her eyes had gone sad when she'd noted that yes, all three kids were hers, though the youngest would resemble little to the other two. They did not share a father, but she'd hoped to raise him to be a better man than her attacker. She'd offered me a place to stay. A place to recover from the brutal infection that had taken over my body, allowing time for the antibiotics to do what they did.

I'd accepted her offer. There was a warmth to Laurel that made me want to stick around. I was still skittish, never able to be around them all at once. Most notably her husband. But they were graceful, treating me as if I were one of their own. Laurel and I grew closer as the weeks went on.

I'd recovered after the first week, but conveniently, either she or I would come up with another excuse to why I couldn't leave just yet. *A storm is coming*, she'd say. *Not enough food to last on my own*, I'd offer the next week, saying I needed more time to gather materials. *Our clothing was stolen,* their oldest daughter, Emma, had stated another week. *Too much fighting in the streets this week*, we'd said on my last week there.

Memories ended my stay abruptly. A nightmare, back to the night *my* world had ended. The day I'd lost it all. Pain seared through my shoulder, snapping me back to reality. Metal chimed against the tiled floors as my katana fell.

A guttural scream rang from my throat. "What? What happened?"

Laurel cradled me, putting pressure on my bleeding wound. They'd shot me. "Tomoe, it's me, honey. It's okay. You were dreaming. Come here, honey, you're going to be okay."

In the distance, a safety clicked, her husband placing

his gun between his waistband and scooping up their now crying kids.

An expression of horror crossed over his features as he finished assessing them for any injuries. "She has to go too, Laurel. I want her gone. Now!"

My body shuddered; tears cascaded down my face. I didn't want to leave. Wasn't ready to.

Laurel cried with me. "I know," she said to us both, and my heart broke.

She patched me up, explaining what my nightmares had taken from me. They'd awoken to the sound of me yelling, screaming over the kids' cots, that they would pay for what they'd taken from me. Not wanting to risk spooking me awake, Laurel had ordered him to take a shot through my shoulder.

A shot he'd very much intended to put through my skull until she'd intervened. She hadn't told me that part, but I could tell. He was about as okay with my presence as I was with his.

"I could have loved you like you were one of my own," she said after moments of silence.

I scoffed, not needing her to try to soften the blow. "I find myself being the product of many possibilities. My world is filled with nothing but 'could,' Laurel. I understand why I have to go."

"It's not what I want. But..." She hesitated. "It's no longer safe for you to stay."

For them. Not for me.

I looked at the woman that had helped me. Saved me. The woman I'd grown attached to. "I understand."

"There's a settlement out in California," she rushed out. "They call themselves *Monterey Compound*. Heard about it from some travelers a few weeks back. It's stable. Under good leadership. There are young people there, people your age. I think you should go."

"If you think I belong there, then I was never close enough to you to be one of your own."

Laurel glared at me from the side of her eye, knowing my words were bullshit. "It will be good for you. You need to heal, Tomoe, need to be around people your own age. Have a shot at doing normal things. Don't you think you deserve a chance to feel safe?"

"Safety is not a luxury I've been awarded in a very long time." It was true.

I hadn't felt safe in well over a year. The reality was, when your sense of safety was taken from you in your most vulnerable state—in your sleep, when you were surrounded by family—there *was* no such thing as safety. Not for me at least, not ever again.

"Well, maybe it's time that changed."

"What about you all?" I shot back at her. "You don't deserve a shot at safety? What makes me so special?"

"Life out here isn't for everyone, but ... now that I've got Hal here. Gosh, honestly, kid, I haven't felt unsafe in a very long time." She smiled at the thought.

Her second husband had been her saving grace after the sudden death of the first who'd died long before any apocalypse. They'd found each other again out on the road. He'd saved her for a second time, too late to stop the horrible fate bestowed upon her. Damage was already done. But he made damn sure he was there to help her pick up the pieces. They were happy, loved this life. Taking this time to live off the land and see sights that would have taken years to see and days off work.

I knew myself. I'd never feel safe here. Wasn't sure if I was ever capable of feeling that again. But if I didn't at least try something else, I wasn't sure how much longer out there I'd want to last. Bitter goodbyes were exchanged between Laurel and me in the morning. Hal had taken the kids and locked them behind their bedroom door the second the locks on my own door had unlatched. She'd apologized, but I shook it off. Wishing her the best and thanking her for all she'd done.

There were no empty promises of somehow finding each other again. We were not foolish enough to hope for that to be true. This Transient Nation was big, what was the continental US was even bigger. Even if we did survive another day, the chances of crossing paths again were unrealistic.

Two days later, the exhaustion wore on my already tired soul. I laid under the stars, shivering into myself, possessing nothing but the layers of clothes on my back, whatever food fit into my bag, and my katana. The layers were not nearly enough for the cold reservation land.

I'd told myself I wasn't heading toward Monterey, was just letting myself go wherever my feet decided to take me that day. That was before I'd found myself along the border of New Mexico and Arizona. A few minutes of travel west in the morning, and I'd cross territory borders.

Closing my eyes, I willed a vision on just as I'd practiced. Figuring out how I could use my powers had been an agonizing effort on an already weak body. I found myself not caring. There was no longer a benefit in leading a life in the dark.

In the following weeks after my family's death, I blamed myself. Determined I'd been cursed for practicing magic that my mother had spent my life telling me wasn't natural. Kana and I spent hours into the night lost in lore and practice. Our aunt had fallen prey to dark magic years before as a young girl, my mother had told us. Kana had pushed back that she didn't understand.

There was nothing inherently dark about paganism. It was what you made of it, your intentions. What my sister and I were doing was what we'd always been meant to do, what our bodies now rewarded us for doing.

That award winning assumption had changed into believing my visions were something of a curse. A punishment for messing with forces beyond what I could fathom. Leaving me unable to help my family when they'd needed me the most, but still forcing me to watch it play out firsthand.

If I could learn to control my curse, there was a chance I'd be able to turn it into a blessing instead. My eyes flickered and my mind went elsewhere. *I was happy, surrounded by a group of people, only the backs of their heads visible. One with curly hair, the other with long brown wavy hair. We were sitting on a green patch eating food. Curly hair flew back as the group laughed, someone leaning in to take our picture. A picture? Wow. It'd been ages since I'd considered the thought. The scene flickered.*

A man with locs walked next to me in silence on a cobblestone path just as the sun crested over the wall, rising for the day. Then I was sparring with someone, a hand reaching down to my own, the vision changing before I could make out a face once more.

The name Prescott echoed in my head. Another flicker. A tall, lean figured man dipped his cowboy hat in my direction, the only part of his face visible being the sultry smile he tossed my way.

It made sense. My family had been vacationing in Monterey for years. The sea otters and whales captivated my mother's heart. I no longer had a place to call home. No longer had a family. But it seemed as if my mother had set me up to find a new one in her absence.

A New Normal

TOMOE

I had needed some air. The buzzing tavern room was closing in on me, my tolerance for my new environment wavering. I'd arrived at The Compound early this morning, having taken advantage of sunrise to make my final five-mile trek here. There'd been soldiers on patrol on the borders of their lands, letting me pass through after checking my belongings and questioning me several times.

They seemed unsure in their orders, constantly looking at one another, double checking with their comrades out of the corner of their eyes. *So much for safety.* While they'd appeared new to their positions, they were far from untrained. Eyes had been on me through each checkpoint all the way to the front door.

Walking toward the gates with confidence, I

demanded to speak with the person behind the only name my vision had provided. Prescott. He towered over me, deciding not to take a seat as he questioned me in some cookie-cutter intake room.

His face was kind, intentions seeming honest. Fidgeted a lot, but for the most part, put together. I sat through a million questions before he pointed me toward a place to stay, stating he'd check in with me a week from now to figure out a job.

So I spent the day exploring. Taking in the beauty of what Prescott and his people had built, the different cultures reflected throughout the infrastructure and overall design. Outside of these walls was an ugly, cruel world. Yet the people inside were filled with smiles, joy brightening their faces as they went through their daily responsibilities. Moving with calm purpose, very different from the hustle you saw even when traveling throughout Transient Nation.

Evening came, and I found myself following the crowd. Not wanting to miss out on the bustle of the night, the familiar feeling of inclusiveness in a group activity sending thrills throughout my body. It was Thursday, according to someone gathered along the street. And I guess Thursdays around here were a call to the weekend.

A tavern had been far down my list of where I'd expected to end my night. Was pushing my limits of being in an enclosed space with people I didn't know, but the excitement in the air fed my curiosity until the room felt so small, I could no longer take it.

The people. The music. The musky scent filtering through the air. The stickiness of the floor beneath my shoes. It'd been too much. I wasn't ready to leave—just needed a second. Stepping out onto the steps, I practically gasped at the relief from the cool evening air.

My head swiveled at the familiar skunky sweet scent filtering in through my nostrils. A girl around my age stood at the bottom of the steps, staring up at me. Large curls framed her pointed face, bouncing as she took in my appearance, mirroring my own movements.

The sight of her jean shorts and cropped top were still jarring, though I too now sported clean, *normal* clothes. I kept myself still under her gaze, though every bit of me wanted to squirm, feeling exposed without the layers I'd grown accustomed to.

A wild grin pulled across her smooth brown skin. "You look like you could use a pick-me-up."

THE MONTEREY COMPOUND

N
W
THE
DOCKS
FISHING &
AL QUARTERS
EAST
GATE
GARDENS
THE
STABLES
LIVESTOCK

CANADA
SALEM TERRITORY
MEXICO
THE PACIFIC OCEAN

STATE OF THE UNION
THE EXPANSE
THE COVERT PROVINCE
TRANSIENT NATION
THE ATLANTIC OCEAN

Feels Like Home

Amaia

"Hell of a day, Pops. You have another speech in you, or can we all relax now?" I asked Prescott, grinning widely at the beautiful woman next to him.

I adored Luna. She was good for him. Was practical enough to keep him from getting lost in daydreams but tender enough to dream with him. Between him and Jax, someone had to help me bring them down to earth. Today had been fun, though. Long, but fun and certainly worth the food.

It had been a year since war had erupted around us. Put us at the center of chaos and destruction. In our year of peace, came a heavy weight on our souls. Peace was not free. It came at a cost. A high price of no longer recognizing who you had to become to survive. The sacrifices we'd all paid to ensure we could keep all that we'd built—

all that we'd hoped to achieve. It was time to celebrate—the people here deserved it.

While this place had become home for me years ago, it was finally beginning to feel like it. The people that surrounded me day in and day out had become something of a family to me. I'd been an only child, never experienced the smothering joy of the large family I'd grown up wishing for. This, the two sisters and brothers at my side, Jax, Prescott, and Luna—it all seemed so ... right. Comfortable. Their presence was a breath of fresh air that made me think I was safe enough to rest.

Luna's arm wrapped around the back of Prescott's neck and he looked at her like a lovesick puppy. She shook her head, speaking softly into his ear with a childlike giggle.

Reina gagged off to the side. "Bleh, y'all please keep those feelings to yourself."

"What, old people can't have sex?" Tomoe smirked as she bit into her sandwich.

Her humor hit home as Seth coughed a laugh, a matching glimmer in his sea-blue eyes as he met her stare. She glanced down nervously, fixing her posture under his watch. Reina's face lit up with joy as our eyes landed on each other, picking up on the same cues we all had since Tomoe had joined the group a few months ago. The crush those two had on each other was juvenile, at best. Fun to watch at a distance since they both didn't appear intent on acting on it anytime soon.

"Actually." Prescott cleared his throat, the red finally

fading from his cheeks and neck. "We thought you and Jax could make the closing speech."

Jax kissed the corner of my mouth, whispering he'd be right back. I glared at the back of his head, then over to Prescott, before settling on Riley for a plea of help. He fought off a grin, the words of defense forming on his lips as Prescott held up a hand to stop him. Riley shrugged, nodding toward Jax in amusement. His auburn hair blew in the wind as he took off toward the building, ducking underneath some kids playing frisbee. They chased after him and I watched on with a smile at the chase. The group weaved in and out of families sprawled across the lawn, the kids' little legs trying to tag him to no avail.

"It'll be good for morale. There will be a day where I won't be here anymore and someone has to take care of this place—"

"Yeah. A million years from now and after an election," I interrupted Prescott. Public speaking made me queasy. Becoming the general of the damn place was already a lot. Easier than Prescott's job given soldiers had to do everything I said no matter what, but still overwhelming.

"An election that will probably begin and end with the two of you," Luna added, pushing her long black hair behind her golden ear.

"Not if I can help it," I said under my breath as I looked to Tomoe to free me from the conversation.

"Lovely picnic chat," Tomoe said with a mouthful of food. "We should do this more often."

Reina sighed, laying back to admire the sky. "Death this. Death that. God, y'all are so morbid, I don't know how we're friends."

"Considering there ain't anyone around here begging to be your friend, I'd expect more appreciation for the group." Seth removed his hat, brushing back his red hair slick with sweat before replacing it on his head.

"Come on," Riley nudged me, a small smile breaking his usual neutral expression. "Live a little. Go. I got your six."

Reina rolled to her knees, cheese and salsa smeared around the edges of her mouth. "Wait, I'll come with you. Just let me finish this taco."

We'd gone all out for the event. Harvesting everything we could spare, we had encouraged our residents to gather in The Kitchens early this morning and challenged them to make the meals they missed the most. Ingredients allowing, of course. The tacos had been a big hit, Reina eating at least five on her own.

"I think the taco is finishing you more than anything," Prescott teased.

"What?" Reina asked, the situation having gotten worse as she stuffed the last half into her mouth. Luna reached over with a napkin, wiping Reina's face while choking back a laugh. "Okay, I'm ready. Off we go, lovebug."

"Hold up, not without a photo. Get close. Ladies first," Jax called, making his way back to us with an old camera we'd found on our last trip outside the walls.

"Ew, no. My hair is crazy," Reina said, toying with her long brown hair and smacking her cheeks gently until they turned a rosy pink. She stopped and took in Tomoe before reaching over to fix her braid. Tomoe smacked her hand away playfully before leaning away and forcing Reina to sprawl against my lap. "Get back here. You need to look good for the camera!"

I scowled at the camera. Jax peered over the lens. "Smile pretty, Mai. The world needs to see it."

The sound of a teasing gag sounded by Riley and Prescott. They exchanged a knowing glance as I bit down my grin. Seth pushed to his feet, lifting Reina upright by her shirt as he walked off toward the tables full of festival foods. Taking a look around, it was hard to contain a true smile. In truth, I was happy to be here. Happy for all I'd survived, in all I'd created, and what the future had in store. Forever. This was the forever I had to look forward to.

Everything from before didn't matter anymore. Who we all were, what we had become after ... that was all I could focus on to keep moving forward. There were two Amaias. The Amaia before the world ended; the soft one, the one that laughed carefree, the Amaia who cared about trivial things like wedding colors and finding the next trendy restaurant to try. Then there was who I'd fought to become. Killed to become. The Amaia that did what she had to in order to survive. There was no going back. There were two versions of us all. Who we were Before and who we'd become After. In The After, the only thing that mattered was keeping the people around me alive and happy. Doing what we could to build anew.

"On the count of three." Jax held up a finger to count down. "Everyone say ispíní."

Reina kept a smile but peered over at me from the corner of her eye as I fell into a fit of laughter at a joke that had become our own. In that moment, I was grateful for the blinding flash of the camera, capturing a memory I wished I could live through a million times.

First Friend

Alexiares

Forty-eight hours.

The outer parts of Chicago lasted a hell of a lot longer than I would have figured. Joliet was fucked from the first hour, Waukegan a day later. All of Aurora followed nearly a week after, once everyone realized there was no coming back from this. The farther out we walked, the more areas we found that had remained relatively civilized considering the conditions.

That wasn't the truth of our situation anymore. Three people had been murdered in the night within the neighborhood we'd shacked up in. No one had heard shit. I didn't let us stick around long enough to find answers. A lack of answers was something I had forced myself to be comfortable with these past two days. The only definitive thing I knew was that bombs had dropped, and we were all fucked.

I wrapped my shirt around my knuckles, forming a fist with my hand. It was dark out now and we needed a place to crash. The walk from Naperville to Schaumburg had almost killed us. We couldn't run forever. We needed shelter, food, a place to rest up and come up with some sort of plan. Schaumburg was good for the short term, but this much radiation couldn't be good for anyone. The wind had picked up, sweeping out radiation disguised as the dust of the remnants of Chicago.

"Stay out here, I'll clear, then signal," I ordered, lining myself up with the class window on the door.

Life had humbled us a lot recently. Just because the place looked like no one was there didn't mean it was empty. With the windows not boarded and from what I could tell, there wasn't any movement inside. Worst-case scenario, there was one of the undead shits lingering in a room upstairs.

Evander's fingers clutched the grip of his gun. "I'm coming in. I'll cover you."

"Don't need your help."

Even though I hated the thought of my brother having to kill someone before everything fell apart, it was the harsh reality we faced now. At this moment in time, however, he was a liability. Evander had gone from creeping up to my height, to toggling the line of seven feet tall. Almost a foot overnight.

His other senses had sharpened too, the sound of my heartbeat keeping him up at night in close quarters. The coppery smell of blood and toxins in the air damn near drove him mad. It was the height that failed us the most. He wasn't yet used to the new proportions of his body. His clumsiness would be of no help for whatever the hell may be inside this house. There had been no sign of me developing any new capabilities, no change in my stature or senses.

I was a ticking fucking time bomb. It wouldn't surprise me at all if I turned into one of the zombie shits. The only thing that mattered now was getting Evander somewhere safe for when I was gone. The window shattered, and we paused, waiting for any movement inside. I stepped in, Evander taking a step inside. He closed his door behind me, gun raised and ready to fire.

"I told you to wait outside."

"And I told you that I have your back." He planted his feet, leaning his back against the door to hold his position in case someone tried to follow us inside.

I shook my head. Clearing this house was the first priority, arguing with him could wait.

"Fine. But stop pointing your gun in my direction."

The downstairs was clear. I moved through it swiftly, thankful for the pile of groceries still on the counter. Whoever had lived here never had the chance to put them away. I tried not to think about who the sorry son of a bitch was. It was better that way. Easier.

Evander kept his place by the door as I edged up the steps. A creak sounded from the room down the hall. I drew my knife, not wanting the ringing of a gun to draw more attention than necessary. I crept down the hallway, pushing open the two doors on either side. A little girl's room decked out in princess shit and what looked to be a spare room. They were clear, though I'd need to double back to check the closets and bathrooms inside.

Taking a shaky breath, I pushed the sole remaining door in. A gun cocked in my face as the man on the other side of the barrel held it with shaky hands. I knew enough from my time working under my father to say confidently that a nervous man with a gun was a man that would shoot.

The whole argument of "guns don't hurt people, people hurt people," had always been fucking stupid to me. The truth lay somewhere in the middle. Unstable people hurt people, and more times than not, the instability resulted in an overreaction. Nerves were lethal, the response to fear and desperation made people do anything to make sure they were the ones to survive.

I dropped the knife, the sound clanging against the wooden floor, hands going up as an indication of waving a white flag.

"Everything okay up there?" Evander called from downstairs.

The man motioned for me to answer his call, gun

waving in my face. I planned on doing that, anyway. No need to drag him up the steps to get his head blown off too.

"Going fine, dropped my knife. Keep watch."

Crouching low, I ducked off to the side, landing a firm grip on his wrist. A risky move, but the idiot didn't even have his finger on the trigger. He was quick, dropping the gun, instead lighting his hands in flames.

A little girl peered around the corner. Tears falling down her bronze skin, not a muffle of a cry leaving her fear ridden mouth. The man's hand flickered, and he released his grip before the flames could burn me. I shuffled for my knife, but he beat me there, a wild look in his eyes.

It slid across the floor, back out of reach. I put my fists up. For what reason? Who the fuck knows? The options before me were a bullet or fire. Fists would do me no good. Panic seized my veins at my lack of power. Recognition filled the man's crazed stare.

Evander burst through the door at the commotion, gun raised, finger on the trigger.

"Wait," I said, lowering my fists.

I would not let my brother take a life. Not yet. Not before he had to. *Unless* he had to.

The man raised his weapon again, this time moving it between Evander and me. "Late bloomer?" he asked, sweat beading along his hairline.

"Go fuck yourself."

"Language," the man recoiled, a disgusted scowl on his face. "There's a child on board."

The little girl came around the corner, fingers in her mouth, fairy wings strapped to her back. She peered up at me, her tears replaced with an innocent grin.

"Do you take me for someone who enjoys the presence of a small child?"

The little girl giggled, waddling over to me with a slobbery hand. "Papi said if I get lost, the first person I should find is someone covered in marker or with crazy hair."

"Cute." I flinched as her cold spit slapped against my palm.

Evander lowered his weapon, the sweat beading against the tip of his nose. He wiped it with the back of his wrist, feet shifting back and forth.

"You lost?"

I studied the man, the question not one I was prepared to answer. He was around my age, his hair cropped low against his head. Brown eyes hardened as mine locked on them, waiting for an answer.

"Hard to be lost when you got nowhere to go," I said.

Evander scowled at me. *Rule #1,* I'd explained, *never tell anyone who we are or where we're going.* But here I was, staring at a little girl with fairy wings and a man with honest eyes. I'd learned the difference years before this. Had to if my plans to ruin my father's plans were to go off without a hitch.

"Same," he mused.

Not shit was funny about our situation. Not even remotely. At the same time, everything was funny because in a blink of an eye, the life we'd known before this had become pointless.

Huffing a laugh, I scanned the room. "Thanks for sharing," I mumbled.

The pair had pitched together a fort out of pink blankets, what appeared to be every pillow in the house underneath it on the floor. Picture books sat atop their makeshift palette, graham crackers and a juice box tipped over on the side.

That wasn't what caught my attention. The stack of canned goods forming a pyramid my height in the corner is what did it. That and the dozen jugs of water in front. They must have been camped up in this room, but to have this much food and water at once ... he was either extremely prepared, or not as honest as he seemed.

"You welcome," the man said, making his way across the room. "Hungry? We have food."

He handed me what appeared to be some sort of jerky in a plastic bag. My nostrils pulled, lips grimacing.

Putting up a hand, I pushed it away. "No thanks, we've seen The Walking Dead."

"Promise it's store bought." He smirked, walking to place a hand on the little girl's shoulder. "The good kind."

"Papi said I can't watch that show with him till I'm older." Her frizzy hair was wild around her face, the brown of her eyes the same as his.

I glanced down. "You make it a habit to talk to strangers?"

"Yes."

Her toothless smile was wide. The sight of it triggering an emotion inside me that I'd fought to bury long before the end of the world. Hope glistened in her small little face, something I hadn't expected to see ever again. I wondered if they'd made it through the last week unmarred, unknowing of what was left out there with the rest of humanity. The darkness that lingered around every corner.

"Well, you should stop," I grumbled, cracking my neck.

It was the man who responded, no doubt trying to intervene before I shattered what normality remained in this child's life. "Why?"

"Because things have changed," I said, taking a step back to stand near my brother. "It's not whatever the hell you thought it was when you holed yourself up in here."

"Name's Tiago, and this is Dahlia. See, now we aren't strangers."

"That's not how that works." I scoffed, an amused sneer replacing the neutral front I'd displayed.

He nodded toward the door in response. "Then get out."

Evander's hand tightened around the grip of his gun. I placed a hand out in front of him, diffusing the situation before his impulsivity put us in an unfavorable situation. While we needed what Tiago had to survive, he had his daughter to worry about. The fight would be a battle of will. I wasn't in the mood to find out who'd come out victorious.

"Yeah, not happening." Evander's face reddened. I was losing control over the situation. On top of the already tiresome teenager hormones, I now had to deal with a second phase of puberty and it was kicking my ass.

"Okay then," Tiago surmised, holstering his pistol and picking the girl up as if they were leaving a damn play date. "Settle in. We hit the road in the morning. You can either come with us, or we can hit the road and part ways. Or you can stay here and give survival your best shot. Either way, we can't take all the food with us, so grab what you need. Leave the rest for whoever needs this place next."

"Hit the road to where?" I asked.

If there was some place safe he knew about, I needed to know where. Maybe it would give Evander a chance. He needed security for when I was gone. And if I couldn't make the trip, then maybe Tiago could get him there himself.

"Up north." His voice was confident, though he didn't grant us with an exact location. "If we hit the border, it'll be better up there."

"The fuck is up there?"

"With our luck," Tiago and the little girl closed in on us, his eyes revealing the honest man beneath. "Everything we've been missing the last week."

"My brother doesn't believe in luck." Evander laughed.

"Me neither." Tiago grinned. "But now seems like a great time to start."

Black Dahlia

ALEXIARES

Dahlia died two-hundred and forty-two days after the bombs dropped. Turned into one of them. The undead in the middle of the night.

We'd thought we were safe. In the home stretch to the promise of a fresh start. St. Cloud, Minnesota had a solid group with decent resources, some semblance of what society used to be. Dahlia had shown no signs of magic in the months we'd spent together. None of us had been concerned. She was young, maybe whatever happened somehow didn't affect young kids. It wasn't like we had any around us to compare her to.

My gifts had fully emerged a few months onto the road. By that point, we'd thought it was the end of the time one could turn. Any stragglers we'd met on the road had a gift of some sort. If only we'd known what was still possible ... if only we hadn't let our guard down.

Choking down any tears, I leaned over to cut the woven bracelet Dahlia had crafted together only a few hours before. Tiago's hand fell in front of my face as I handed it to him. Sputtered, tearful coughs erupted from him as his knees gave out, his grief overwhelming him. I placed a hand on his back in offer of support. Someone had to keep it together right now. If we both lost ourselves to grief, we wouldn't survive.

What reason is there for you to live? Your purpose is right in front of you, clinging to life.

Blood dribbled down the side of Evander's mouth, his hand twitched out to the side, clutching for a grasp on life.

"Please," he managed to sputter. My brother's fingers found the thigh of my pants and tugged ever so slightly. "Please. Survive."

No. He was not trying to find a way to hold on. Instead, he was asking for me to let him go.

"He's suffering," Tiago murmured. "Ay dios, he's suffering."

"I have eyes," I bit out.

It was unfair. It wasn't his fault his daughter had killed my brother. It was mine.

Only I could be of blame for the losses that I suffered. It was my fault my mother wasn't here. I hadn't held on tight enough. The loss of my brother was on me too. I should have never let us get too comfortable. Deep down, I knew what the possibilities were. Without a definitive answer on what happened with children, keeping my guard down was irresponsible.

Our father may have been a sack of shit, but at least the life skills he'd instilled in us had a purpose. And like a prophet from hell, Alexander Drakos had predicted the inevitable: my carelessness would lead to the demise of my family. My brother.

Evander's trembling hand fell to the grip of his gun. He'd attempted to pull it on her but hadn't had the strength to pull the trigger. None of us had until it was too late. Then Tiago had done what only he had the authority to do ... put Dahlia out her misery for she would not have wanted to live that way.

There weren't many memories I shared with my grandparents. Our father's parents had died before we were born and our mother's, well, Alexander had ensured we had little to no contact. Yiayia would watch after us only when our father was away during our summer trips to Mykonos.

"That one's been here before," she would say as she *watched Evander interact with the world.*

The same could be true for Dahlia. She was young, but she was wise beyond her years and had been well adapted to life in the middle of an apocalypse. Ending up like the undead had terrorized her in her dreams. Even if Evander hadn't been a factor, putting her down would have been what she wanted.

It was what my brother was asking for in this very moment. Regret washed over me as I slid the gun from underneath his pale blue hand. Nodding my head, I took in the shell that was becoming my brother. His eyes flickered with emotion, the journey of our brotherhood flashing between us both. Choking on tears, I brought my forehead down against his and scooped up the bloodied teddy bear off the ground.

It was the last thing Evander had bought before his world shattered. He'd meant to give it to the daughter of our father's associate at the funeral. The teenage crush he'd had on her kept him from handing it over, along with the guilt of knowing what our father had done. Ultimately, he'd decided to leave it at home. Why it was one of the few items he'd chosen to pack before we'd left the home tied to so many terrible memories, I wasn't sure. I tucked it against his side.

A whisper of a touch brushed the back of my head. Evander's finger fell onto my shoulder in his weakened state. "It's okay," he said.

There were a million things I wished for at that moment. Saving my brother wasn't one of them. In the here, the now, the only thing I wished I could change were the final months we'd had together. I'd wasted a shit ton of time trying to harden him up. *Tough love,* I'd explained when Tiago suggested I loosened the reins, tried a softer approach with him. He hadn't seen Evander's softness as a weakness, instead he'd seen it as something that gave him hope.

I hadn't viewed it that way. There wasn't a way humanity could recover from this. Not in our lifetime. It didn't mean civilization was gone, over with. It just meant we had to start from ground zero. That was what I'd have to leave my brother with if something happened to me. So I did my best to shape him, mold him into what I thought it took to survive in a world that looked like … this. Like death.

Only now, as I watched on in his final breaths, did I realize that in the attempt to save my brother's life, I'd become the person we'd hated the most. Our father.

"I'm sorry I was never the brother that you deserved. I'll do better for the both of us, I promise." Tiago jumped at the sound of the gunshot echoing through the breaking dawn.

The Making of The Bloodhound

ALEXIARES

"Keep moving, my friend." Tiago's hand fell on the top of my pack.

The trees that lined the highway were dying. Teardrops of frost hung from their branches. Glass from the shattered windows of abandoned cars crunched under his boots as he passed me. Here we were, St. Cloud. This was our end goal. So why didn't the ease of comfort overwhelm me as I stood before a sign telling us where to go?

"You go ahead, I'll catch up."

Tiago halted up ahead, a tease of a smile pulling at the corner of his mouth. It was the best he could do since Dahlia. Since Evander. "If I listened to every lie that came out of your mouth, we would have never become friends."

"Who said we're friends?" I asked, still not moving from where I'd come to a stop.

The pink lining the sky was misleading. A beautiful ending to a day filled with darkness. It felt like we took turns being the strong one, trying to keep the other going. Today was his turn. It had been mine the last week. I just couldn't quite bring myself to care. Without Evander, I wasn't sure what the hell I was doing this for. Tiago was strong. He didn't need me to survive.

That wasn't what friendship was. He was the first friend I'd ever had, but had taught me a lot during our time on the road. Friendship wasn't built on need—it was built on want. I *wanted* to be there for him. Wanted to make sure he would be okay. So I'd followed him to the only place we knew to go.

"If you want to be more than that, I'm afraid I'm going to have to ask you to buy me dinner first." He swooped in behind me, pushing on the back of the head and over toward the clear path on the road. "This is it. A new start." Hope glistened in his eyes for the first time in months.

"Doesn't seem like much," I grumbled honestly. We needed to tamper our expectations, keep them realistic.

He sighed, irritated at the consistent negativity I'd been feeding into the 'universe.' The whole manifestation kick he was on was starting to get on my damn nerves. Where had hoping for food or shelter gotten us lately?

"Enough, Alexi. It's getting colder, and it does not appear that it's going to warm up anytime soon." Tiago motioned to the barren tundra leading to the city. "Look around. It's supposed to be nearing spring. Do you see anything other than trees? Any blooms, *animals*? We need food, a roof over our heads. Some sort of consistency. This could be the last stop for us. Don't make me go in alone, man. Me and you. We're in this together."

I glanced toward my friend. He was right—we had nothing to lose but our lives. After the losses we suffered, that wasn't necessarily a bad thing to either of us. Tiago had warmed up to me early on. It was easy for him to share the details of his personal life. Our first night together, the phone lines had cut on for a moment.

The raw, agonizing, pain filled yell that had escaped him when he realized his brother was gone was so familiar, yet foreign to me. I hadn't ever felt that strongly about the death of a loved one. Even with my mother, her loss stung, sure, but she'd never really been a mother to me. It wasn't until Evander until I'd recognized it for what it was; your soul shattering. Breaking. Tearing a wound irreparably deep.

What I'd come to appreciate about Tiago was his will to go on. He was relentless in his decision to keep going, to keep moving forward. Though he posed it as if he was doing me a favor, I knew when it came down to it, he himself wanted to survive. He wanted to live, no matter how much the guilt haunted him. It was a tough thing to process. But I feared that if he lost one more person, he may not see things that way anymore. As any good friend would, I followed him through the tangled maze of cars toward the new beginning he was hoping for.

We heard her first. The eerie sound of a woman

singing. Her voice ricocheted off metal sculptures stacked with sharp objects meant to impale. She danced around the traps, her focus on angling glass near the base to reflect the sun.

The woman halted in her steps and pulled out a Walkman. Ducking behind the sculpture closest to us, our breathing hitched as we kept watch, scoping out the situation. There was no one else around. The walls up ahead were incomplete in most areas. Though a metal slab of a gate blocked the main road in, everything beyond it was absent of life. Her singing continued as we shifted back onto the path inside.

She tensed the moment she sensed our approach. Like idiots, we'd closed in on her unarmed. The consequences came quick as she drew her weapon from her holster in the blink of an eye. Blonde hair surrounded her pointed face resembling a golden halo. Ice-blue eyes met mine, creasing at the sides from her wicked grin.

"Woah," Tiago said, taking a slow step forward with his arms out in front of him. "We aren't zombies, relax."

With all our layers, who knew what the fuck she saw us as. The only thing you could make out for certain was a small sliver of our faces. I'd stopped being able to feel my legs fifty miles and one week ago.

Her laugh was chirped, not quite a giggle yet sinister all the same. "I know." She holstered her gun, tossing her hair back over her shoulders.

Tiago took a slow, deliberate look at our surroundings, his eyes finally settling on the woman. She was reading him too. The way her gaze lingered on every detail in an attempt to decode him. His eyes flickered over her face, narrowing at the slight tension in her shoulders.

"¿Qué te pasa?" I asked, wondering if he saw something that I did not.

"Este lugar," he mumbled, his hands motioning to the deserted landscape. "Está mal. Algo no anda bien."

Sure, it wasn't what I expected of the so-called promise land we'd heard about on the road, but maybe it was just a front to keep those not wanted away. "¿Te gustaría explicar más?"

"Where is everyone?" Tiago asked her, cutting to the chase.

She shrugged, her pretty eyes wavered over to me, the whites around her iris slightly unsettling even at a distance. "Not here, obviously."

"Look around, Alexiares," Tiago tried to reason with me. "Debería haber gente. Todo parece abandonado."

We'd kept to ourselves for the most part, but from what I'd seen during my time with my friend, hesitancy to accept a new face was out of character. The fear of attachment preventing him from seeing things clearly. This place wasn't about scenic landscapes or the buzz of society, it was about survival. For what purpose, hell if I knew. The only thing that I was certain of was that Tiago was set on living, and St. Cloud was the opportunity for him to do so.

"Si ella está aquí sola, supongo que es más seguro que

cualquier otro lugar en el que estemos solos," I said, seeing the logic in what he wanted to assume as a threat.

An objectively beautiful woman that felt safe enough to be alone meant there was little to fear. That was good, wasn't it? Trying to read into the finer details had become a habit for the two of us. Missing those smaller signs had only led to life ending consequences before, but maybe there was a point when too much skepticism could produce the same damning results.

Tiago shook his head, not seeing things the same way. "Yes. Ella está aquí sola, ella es la amenaza."

Piercing blue eyes drilled into Tiago who remained unfazed. Even in his grief, the gravity of seriousness that reflected in his features was unnatural. I watched the two of them, curious about how the situation would play out. If we weren't allowed to stay, I'd go with him, but as I studied the woman, I found her attitude oddly captivating. There was a defiant spark in her gaze, a casual confidence that was both intriguing and refreshing. It stirred something deep within me, something primal akin to flight or fight.

She couldn't understand what we were saying and didn't try to hide it. Her wicked expression was unmasked and genuine. The absence of fear in her struck me. For the first time, someone looked at me without any hint of fear. The rarity of it was disarming.

"Earphones on, all alone. Her senses cut off. We can't trust this," Tiago said in a hushed tone.

"Is there a problem, boys?" she asked, twirling the

blonde hair underneath her beanie. "Not what you were expecting?"

Tiago retreated, refusing to give her his back. "We're mistaken. Our apologies. We did not mean to startle you."

A frown of genuine confusion consumed her round lips. "Why would I be startled?" She closed the gap between us once more. There was a swagger in her gait when she moved. Slowly, she tore her icy gaze from my friend and over to me. It felt like the first time she truly noticed me as her eyes trailed over me. Marking every detail. "There's only two of you. I've taken more with less."

I gripped Tiago's arm, holding him in place. Over the last few weeks, we'd done our best to cover our bases, explore our options from the corners of towns we passed through and homes we lingered outside of. This was as safe as the world was going to get. We wouldn't get another chance at this. "You got a name?"

"Finley," she winked, biting down on her bottom lip. Her golden hair whipped in the wind with the toss of her head toward the city. "Don't you forget it, sweetheart."

"Maybe if you paid closer attention to instructions, your only friend wouldn't be dead."

"Finley!" Cael slammed his fist against the long table in the center of Finley's lab.

"*Dad,*" she mocked, a shrill cackle passing through her

viscous red lips. "What? Is telling the truth such a bad thing? He needs to hear this, and maybe he won't kill the next one he makes."

I winced. It still hurt though over a year had passed. The truth more times than not stung. There was no point in finding sadness in her words, for I had no one to blame but myself, and the one person I would give anything to have a chance to kill. I deserved this pain. Embraced it. Pain was weakness, but it was also bliss.

"I followed your orders to the letter, Finny," I ground out. She'd been in a mood for over a month and I was growing tired of being on the receiving end of her cruelty.

Finley had two sides to her: hot and cold. She was either vindictive and angry, or calm and collected. Never sweet, but genuine in a way that made it easy to forgive some of her worst moments. I'd been through worse, and she only inflicted what I allowed. It eased the pain of some of the harder memories. The ones that made me scream in the darkness of the night.

She swayed over to me, cupping my chin and planting a soft kiss on my lips. Blonde hair brushed against my cheeks as she pulled back to study me, searching with nothing but ice in her blue eyes. "Yet, you still failed me."

I stared down the bridge of my nose, meeting the eye of the woman who had somehow become my wife. It had all happened so fast. A whirlwind of a year that had resulted in a role I now occupied with no clue on how I'd gotten here. Actually, I could. By not listening to my friend. To turning a back to Tiago and his warnings not only in life, but in his death as well. Had I listened to him two years ago ... *no.* I couldn't let myself think that way. There was no guarantee Tiago would have ever made it this far. *At least you wouldn't have been the one to kill him.*

"Failed your daddy. Failed your mommy. Evander ..." Finley's hands traced the vials filled with blue and clear fluids along the brick walls.

"That's enough." Cael's words were quiet but firm as he pushed up from his stool. He grimaced slightly at the movement. Just barely distinguishable from the usual jerkiness, but enough for me to notice it, along with the cough he now attempted to cover with the constant clearing of his throat. "What's done is done, Finley. Let it rest in the past and focus on how to move us forward."

"Our people are starving," Finley reasoned, her tone sliding into one of a spoiled brat who wasn't getting her way. "I *am* focusing on how to move us forward. Had my disappointment of a husband managed to secure our next resource from Madison, we'd be one step closer to that goal. Instead, he lost them to ... What was it this time— Gunfire? Molotov cocktail?—outside St. Paul. *Again.* After I specifically told him to avoid that barbaric little wasteland. Which by the way, common sense would tell you to find a new route considering you've lost three out of the last eight I sent you to fetch."

It was a paradox really. How I could find such thrill in the sound of her voice, a small, pathetic tendril of comfort, yet hate it all the same. No matter how hard I tried or the crazy shit she put me through, I couldn't figure out how to stop loving the woman on the other end. That's what love was though, messy. A choice you had to make daily. *Work* is what my mother always described it as.

One moment the two of us were casually hooking up in the late nights at her lab and the next she was calling me her husband. The bronze ring on my left hand burned with my irritation. It was hard to find love in a symbol that had only woven us together in a way that confined me, trapped me ... suffocated *me*. She would help me control my magic, the power that had killed the last sliver of good within me along with my best friend. But not without a cost. Her help was conditional, and the other nine silver rings on my fingers proved that. Our weeks of fun were short-lived. Finley couldn't keep up her facade for long.

Before the hookups had been the shameless bouts of flirtation she'd sent my way to the disapproval of none other than Tiago. He always had a way of convincing me to take a step back to evaluate, not try to settle down, especially with the *she-devil*. He'd called her that from the first day we'd met her in what felt like forever ago. After the war had been different. I needed another constant in this life that always seemed to be changing.

"Did you, babe?" I rolled my eyes. "Sorry, instructions were unclear over your screeching and—"

"Dammit." Cael's pale fingers wrapped around his cane. He slammed it into the floor then hobbled over to his daughter. She was the opposite of him in every way.

"There is one enemy here yet the two of you will tear each other's throats apart before they have a chance to strike next."

She brushed him off. Ignoring the pit that place had put us in since war. What they had taken from us. From me. "I'm not worried about that little bitch from Monterey. She's down there and our people are up here. As long as she remains there, then she is none of our concern. They're weak. I give it another year before their *society* falls apart. No need to waste our efforts on drawing her out. This life isn't meant for them, we're safe."

"Safety is a state of mind, Finley," Cael reminded her with utmost patience. "It's not real. I've taught you that."

"I understand the sentiment but I'm focusing on the facts. Look, I've run the numbers, AquaXelium is far beyond my scope of abilities, gifts or not. Even the best know when to take on a mentor, someone more ... specialized in their expertise."

"Mentor." I huffed a laugh, propping an arm against the counter in the corner to take in another one of her lies.

Cael was a decent man, but he willfully blinded himself to who his daughter had become. Sometimes the old her slipped through, or who I assumed she may have been before life happened. Lately though, that girl seemed gone, replaced with someone who was consumed in testing science and pushing the limits of what was possible with a touch of magic.

The pleasure she found in her mishaps was mildly

concerning to the sane individuals of St. Cloud. It was why no one ever questioned her. Not even me. She glared at me, the promise of her rage later demanding my silence.

"What is he talking about?" Cael asked, staring at me with a different, more favorable punishment if I didn't comply.

I could always leave. I thought about it on every mission she sent me on outside our borders. In the end, I always returned. Where else could I go? Everywhere. Anywhere. That was the answer. I could disappear without a trace tomorrow and Finley would never find me.

It was the entire point of the role she'd forced me into taking, preying on the sinister thoughts that lingered in the back of my mind. She saw the darkness that was instilled in me from a young age and nurtured it, molding me into her little pet. *The Bloodhound*, or so they called me.

Truth was, I didn't leave because I was a coward. What would I have left to feel if Finley did not exist? The highs and lows of life would no longer be, only lows would remain and I wasn't sure if I could handle that. Not with my own promises I'd made to Evander and Tiago in the wake of their deaths.

Finley was rash, occasionally cruel when she got worked up. Some of her morals were questionable, sure, but in the end her actions boiled down to one thing; passion. She only wanted to form a settlement full of survivors and to do that, we had to survive. That goal had never changed for as long as I'd known her.

She sighed, tucking her hair behind her ear at the sight of me prepared to reveal her secrets. Finley could do her best, but nothing would hurt more than knowing that my best friend, my only friend, had died by my hand. My power.

"I was going to tell you when I was able to get it to work."

"Get *what* to work?" Cael pressed.

"Collective conscious," Finley explained what she was attempting to achieve. "If I get the smartest and brightest in one place, create a network that merges into a single mind, we can achieve the impossible. St. Cloud will be unstoppable."

"This mind being whose, Finley?"

"Hers," I grumbled in response.

She glared at me. "Well, who else would it be? Our people will be better for it."

Eyes dark as night widened in horror. "No. It's not right. These are people, Finley. Innocent children!"

"There is no innocence in this world, daddy, not anymore. It's a small sacrifice to make for the greater good." She reached for her father, halting his retreat as he stepped away from her in fear. Finley recognized it for what it was—her father seeing her as everyone else did for the first time. Her bottom lipped wobbled in defense the way it always did when she knew she was fighting a losing battle. "It's a good plan. It can work. Think of all the problems we have. Our people could be set for life! Two minds are better than one."

Cael's head moved from side-side, his eyes scanning the room until they landed on me. I stared back at him, my expression no doubt void of any emotion. I disagreed with Finley's method, but I was in no place to interfere further. I'd done my part. Saved who I needed to save and killed who I didn't. I had to think about myself too. The repercussions of my actions. If I gave up this life, this home, then everything was all for nothing. Then *they* died for nothing.

"You can't be okay with this?" he asked me, pleading with me to try to reason with a woman who didn't take kindly to peer feedback.

I fought to remain neutral no matter how much I wanted to meet his stare with a gaze of understanding. I'd felt myself getting attached at the onset of our working relationship, right after the war. His eyes trailed down to the rings I was teasing along my fingers then back to my face. Regret washed over his features.

Of course I wouldn't say anything, I'd been an experiment for Finley too. Still was with her having yet to find the solution to the problem she had promised to solve. I was no fool. She could if she wanted to. But that was not how Finley worked. Without power, without an edge over those around her, she would unravel. If I didn't follow her orders, she would take what little control I did have.

Cael cleared his throat, glancing back in her direction. "One more," he said, making his way to the door. He stood there for a moment, taking a deep sigh with his back to us. "One more and if it doesn't work, we end this, Finley."

"You know, you should consider yourself lucky." A massive Cane Corso lurked at my heels, jaws snarling and lined with drool.

Extended assignments had their perks. The ability to bring Suckerpunch along was, by far, the best one. I'd found him as a puppy right outside the city and in a rare lapse of caution, the little devil had taken on a zombie in my defense. He'd barely been the size of my head at the time but his heart had been mighty. The heart of a warrior, a survivor. So I'd kept him against Finley's wishes.

In the center of a bed in a dilapidated room, a terrified, sorry excuse of a man trembled uncontrollably. I suppose I should have been thankful to him. The weeks tracking him down had given me the space to clear my head. Figure out what I wanted. If he hadn't been on the run, who knew if the opportunity to do so would arise? *Running from the Bloodhound*, I laughed to myself. An ironic name considering Finley hated dogs.

He'd stolen from Finley and Finley hated thieves. *Use your best discretion*, she'd advised for dealing with him. The designs he'd taken with him had been classified—a project she'd been working on for ages. Two hours and a very long, drawn out round of torture later and he'd revealed he'd burn them.

"Wh-why?" he stammered out, the blood along his nail bed finally clotting to a halt.

I sighed, taking a seat in the chair directly across from him. "Because over the last few days, I've decided I don't want to do this anymore."

Venting to a dead man was freeing. The comfort of knowing your words would be lost to the soil, buried with the dead.

"You're not going to kill me?" A pitiful amount of hope pooled in his eyes. Nothing could have made me want to kill him more. Hope was a stupid fucking thing to have in the world in which we lived.

Laughing, I gave Suckerpunch a pat on the head. "I didn't say that, now, did I?" Suckerpunch grinned up at me, the drool around his mouth dripping onto the moldy carpet.

The man's teeth clattered, the sound grating the last tendrils of my nerves. He winced as the sheets touched the sensitive skin on the cauterized wounds of his missing toes. "Then what do you mean?"

"You're my last kill," I said, my words clipped as if it couldn't be more obvious. "Can't keep doing this. Guess you can say the old hound is going into retirement."

"You said I was lucky."

Scooting my chair closer to the side of the bed, I leaned over him with scrunched brows as he sunk into the mattress. Tears tumbled down his face, the blubbering of his whimpers growing louder with each passing minute.

"Well, I'm a lot of things, but I'm not a liar. Here's the deal. I need leverage. So, you're going to give me the information I need to earn my freedom. See these rings here?" I asked, holding my hand in front of his face. "Are our gifts really gifts if in the end they cause our downfall? I mean to be powerful is a beautiful, beautiful thing. The consequences of having this much however, can be brutal. Devastating. Makes you do shit that keeps you up at night. Recently I've come to the conclusion that I just want peace."

His cries turned into the torturous wail of a dead man. Backing into the wall behind the bed, he fell silent, the realization of nowhere to hide rooted him in place.

"You're a great listener, you know that? Feels like a real bonding moment here. Tell you what, I'll make your death quick." I flashed him a toothy grin. "But first, I need you to tell me everything you know about Monterey Compound. And before you open your stammering mouth to lie to me, I know that's where you're headed. I found your map."

"You're About To Find Out."

ALEXIARES

"Out of the tree, son."

The voice startled me. Considering not much else did these days, I took it as a sign to listen to the old man glaring up at me with piercing eyes. Caught red-fucking-handed, *Bloodhound* wasn't a name I carried around lightly. It had been hard earned and heavy worn. I'd moved through countless territories undetected for so fucking long I'd started to believe myself a ghost.

While it wasn't the first time the unfortunate had happened, I hadn't expected it to happen here. I'd been watching them for days. The Monterey Compound territory was well-covered, but not as impenetrable as it'd been made out to seem.

More, it appeared, was the only thing keeping this place standing for their notorious general had been absent from what I could tell. Granted I couldn't see much in this tree, and I'd be an idiot to expect to see her gallivanting beyond the walls on her own. Pain shot up my ankles as my feet connected with the ground. I took a moment to scan the crowd.

The old man hadn't come alone. Two soldiers stood behind him, guns raised, but the confidence in his stance let me know he could hand out an ass whooping or two on his own. We were level eyed though he had at least twenty pounds on me.

I tilted my head with a smirk. "You should really kill on command, would probably have solved your gate problem."

"Who said it was a problem?" His voice was firm, harsher than gravel but calm.

"You don't take me as stupid, old man." I huffed a laugh as I dropped my weapons against the hard soil. "That herd didn't plan that on their own."

The command to disarm had not been explicitly stated. Spend enough time around jumpy businessmen with the itch to kill and the signs become apparent. Each soldier flanking the man kept their stance and hard glares trained on me, but the twitch of their fingers near the trigger had me seeing a new opportunity before me.

A *different* way to get in. To accomplish what I'd come here for.

"If I'm not stupid, then why are you giving me advice on how to handle infiltrators of my Compound?" he asked, approaching me without a care in the world. Dropping down, he scooped up my pistol and knife, tucking them into the waist of his pants.

"You think I did it," I said, my voice steady as I dropped my shoulders in defeat. "I get it. You don't know me. But think about it: if I was a true threat, would I really be standing here unarmed and vulnerable?"

The man grabbed my arm, pushing me out in front of him. No blood splattered his clothing. If I had to guess, he'd been outside their little walls when shit hit the fan.

"If I thought that, you would not be walking by my side," he surmised with a grin.

The lack of uniform had me confused with the way the soldiers looked to him for direction. He wasn't in their military, yet he clearly possessed some level of authority over them. A leader in their community, perhaps.

My mind raced for all that I had learned in preparation for coming to tear this place down. Though I had left St. Cloud in a hurry, I'd spent time on the road gathering intel. I could not defeat an enemy that I did not know. Besides their incompetent general, there were two others who'd help found this haven of which my misery was founded—one by the name of Jax and the other Prescott. Death had called for Jax before I could arrive—a mercy for him no doubt—which meant the one before me was none other than Prescott.

"All that means is you haven't figured it out yet, and you're waiting for the answers to come," I chided, biting down the smirk from the guns poking into my back.

They were right to fear me, *especially* when I was

unarmed. Made me release some ... creative energy I suppose.

"You catch on quick."

Arching a brow, I met his side-eye glance. "Quick enough to be concerning?"

"Precisely." He tilted his head toward the blistering sun with a laugh.

"Smart man."

Metal crunched underneath my boots as we passed through the remains of the gate in silence. *North Gate* if my blueprints had been correct. Prescott said nothing to call off the soldiers marching behind me with their weapons raised. Any hopes of keeping my arrival low-key was thwarted. Every soldier working on cleaning up the mess stared me down with anger simmering eyes. *Enemy.* I knew the look well. Had spent the entirety of my journey determined to learn how to hide it for the day I met their general face to face.

To truly savor her despair, I'd need to get close, play the long game. There was one final assignment I needed to complete before I left this world. I'd be damned if I didn't stop to smell the flowers while doing so.

"Whatever you're leading me to, can't be worse than anything I've gone through. Torture will not work on me."

"What I'm leading you to, *young man*, is far worse than torture." There was a dark humor in his words. Mocking almost. Like he had played that final move in a lengthy game of chess after toying with me long enough for me to relax, to feel victorious—then snatching it away.

The soldiers at our backs snickered, whispering to each other low enough that their words evaded me. There was something going on here. Something that they knew and I didn't. Licking the corners of my mouth, I accepted my fate for what it was.

"What's worse than torture?" I asked, curiosity getting the best of me.

This place tested people. *That* had been the whispered lore lost into the wind and shadows of other settlements. Where I came from, people hated Salem Territory— Monterey Compound specifically. If they didn't hate it, they wanted to be here. More times than not, I found it to be a mix of both. Hated the fact that they couldn't be here *because* of the way it tested you. From what I knew, their gates were open to all. It'd made it easy to conclude that fear of the unknown had kept people rooted in place. Otherwise, why wouldn't they make the trip themselves?

Before I'd arrived, I hadn't known what the hell the words I'd heard in the corners of dark streets and mold-licked taverns meant. 'Test' could mean a lot of things these days. Now, it was clear to me and I'd walked myself right into what I was sure was the first of many tests.

Prescott's eyes glimmered with amusement as he stepped behind me in a swift movement, his hand gripping the back of my neck. "You're about to find out."

Part One
Sneak Peek at
RISING

One

AMAIA

EVERYTHING WAS JUST A THEORY BEFORE THE bombs went off. That's the thing about science. You can only prove so much without a doubt. Until chaos erupts.

I considered myself a woman of science once. Fact over fiction, or opinion, any day. Guess they were right about how life can change in an instant. For thousands of years, humans placed ourselves at the top of the animal kingdom, thinking we were better than all species.

There was a show I'd watched years ago. One of the main characters had stated that the only difference between us and them was opposable thumbs and the ability to have complex language. For a long time, I internalized that.

Thought about it to the point it made my head hurt. He wasn't wrong. If anyone cared to pay attention to the outcome of Chernobyl outside the cancer and outward appearance of the mutated animals, the ridiculous theory on the end of humanity wouldn't have been a theory at all. They thought humanity would be brought to its knees.

Well, evil doesn't die easily. Humanity is … resilient.

Turns out some of us are immune to radioactive bullshit. It's literally in our DNA. The strong ones. The ones Darwin gushed about. The ones that would persevere, no matter the circumstances. The resilient. Some of us have a magic green thumb, some a knack for all things fire, others water. Others possess a scary amount of accuracy with anything that could be considered a weapon. I should know, I'm one of them.

Then there're the Pansies. Though the words amused me, it wasn't the official name. Some say "respect the dead" or whatever. I say to hell with it, they aren't really dead.

Just something else.

Something that borderlines both humanity and beast. An impossibly perfect balance of light and dark. They still think, just not the same as us. They walk and run with impossible speed and grace. The fundamental difference is that they fucking reeked like the dead and eat human flesh.

I was twenty-two when it all happened. Fresh out of university, working at some soul-sucking company. It was miserable but paid the bills. As good as life could be for a young girl in the U. S. of A. The perfect fiancé, the ferocious pup, a core group of friends, nice car, well-funded parents. As a child I'd told myself there was no chance in hell I'd ever be one of those people who spent their whole life behind some stuffy desk. Perhaps I'd spoken the wrong thing into existence.

That was five years ago. A different lifetime. My biggest problem went from mustering the energy to cook for the fourth time that week after a tough workout class to chasing some asshole out of our territory or clearing a field full of Pansies.

It helps clear my head, anyway. I'd always told Jax it's good for people to see the General out in action. Leading from beside them, as one of them. Within them. But the truth was, it helps me get out all the pent-up aggression from living in such close quarters. Enclosed settlements had that effect on people. Big enough for everyone to have their own space, small enough for everyone to know each other and spread your business when there was nothing else to do. Despite it being thirty-thousand people deep.

More times than not, it felt akin to a prison. Like someone was just waiting for a spark to set everything ablaze into flame, then kick the dirt over it and move along, pretending nothing ever happened. Rumors ran rampant throughout The Compound all the time about settlements reforming, joining as one to take over with a military state of mind. Forming some sort of sick alliance with The Pansies.

"Amaia." *Ugh, one day.* For twenty-four hours, I'd asked for a moment of respite. Told everyone to find a hobby outside of bothering me. "Maia. Maia, wake up.

Seriously, what the hell, get up!" I breathed in once, soaking in the last few moments of the warm sun heating my russet skin.

"I'm not asleep. Get off me." I shrugged one of my best friends off. God, she could be persistent.

She was usually the type to respect others' privacy when asked, not wanting to encroach on any boundaries. *This better be urgent.* I opened my eyes to her pale, olive hued skin and dark brown hair.

"You're drunk. God, unbelievable. I shoulda known. Moe was willing to bet she saw you take off with a bottle, but I didn't want to believe her. Said it must be extra water, and you'd gone off on one of your hikes. You're really something you—"

I rolled my eyes and cut her off before her loud voice could ring anymore, rattling my brain.

"I'm not drunk, Reina. I'm simply relaxing my mind, soaking up a moment of peace." We'd spent weeks out securing our borders, the uptick of attacks concerning. I sat up and quickly scanned the old abandoned golf course, now littered with tall grass and patches of trees.

It nestled me between it and the cliff. Most people would never close their eyes in such a precarious situation. Pansies were quick and efficient when they went in for the kill. There'd been many times where someone excused the snapping of a branch as a deer, just to be wrong, and to only have a cliff as an escape route.

Yeah, I could see how that would make people uneasy, but I was just as lethal, just as efficient as they were. Even if

I was half out of my mind thanks to the bottle of tequila now half empty at my side. Most apocalypse shows I saw insinuated a bottle of alcohol or drugs would run dry thanks to those trying to take themselves out of the equation. The writers clearly had no imagination.

If the world was going to shit, best believe man would find a way to continue their escapism.

My eyes narrowed as I took in the sadness on her face. Despite her job, she never let much break her even demeanor. She'd claimed it was to help keep her patients calm, but even as General, I wasn't sure how she could be so *on*, all the time.

The position I held didn't give me the luxury of feeling things. Caring, sure. Dedicated, always. But being emotional was never an option. Which meant I needed to shed the emotions somewhere and why I'd tried to make my peaceful day once a week a priority. Yet somehow, it always ended up ruined.

"Amaia, it's Jax," she huffed. "There's been an accident."

I sprang to my feet, taking off towards The Compound, not bothering to see if Reina could keep pace.

About the Author

Nelle Nikole was born in California, spent time in the battlefields of Virginia, and now lives in Atlanta with her husband Ben and their furkid Sophie. A lifelong reader, she began writing thrilling stories to share with her classmates as early as elementary school. Having lived a little bit of everywhere, Nelle decided to take her studies international and completed her Anthropology degree by researching abroad in Rio de Janeiro and throughout Cuba. Driven by an insatiable appetite for knowledge, Nelle received a Master's degree in Public Policy. Using her studies to influence her work, Nelle finds herself inspired by all things fantasy, apocalyptic and anything in between.

instagram.com/authornellenikole

www.ingramcontent.com/pod-product-compliance
Lightning Source LLC
Chambersburg PA
CBHW072115300726
48975CB00003B/818